THE SCROLL OF CHAOS

THE SCROLL OF CHAOS

ELSIE CHAPMAN

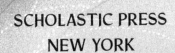

SCHOLASTIC PRESS

NEW YORK

Library of Congress Cataloging-in-Publication Data

Names: Chapman, Elsie, author.
Title: The scroll of chaos / Elsie Chapman.
Description: First edition. | New York : Scholastic Press, 2023. | Audience: Ages 8–12. | Audience: Grades 7–9. | Summary: Twelve-year-old Astrid Xu stumbles upon an ancient Chinese scroll that she hopes is the key to curing her mother's depression, but when it transports her and her younger sister Marilla to a realm where Chinese legends are real, they suddenly find themselves caught in a war between good and evil.
Identifiers: LCCN 2022028281 (print) | LCCN 2022028282 (ebook) | ISBN 9781338803235 (hardcover) | ISBN 9781338803242 (ebk)
Subjects: LCSH: Scrolls, Chinese—Juvenile fiction. | Magic—Juvenile fiction. | Mythology, Chinese—Juvenile fiction. | Good and evil—Juvenile fiction. | Sisters—Juvenile fiction. | Mothers and daughters—Juvenile fiction. | Adventure stories. | CYAC: Scrolls—Fiction. | Magic—Fiction. | Mythology, Chinese—Fiction. | Good and evil—Fiction. | Sisters—Fiction. | Mothers and daughters—Fiction. | Adventure and adventurers—Fiction. | BISAC: JUVENILE FICTION / Legends, Myths, Fables / Asian | JUVENILE FICTION / Family / Siblings | LCGFT: Action and adventure fiction. | Fantasy fiction. | Novels.
Classification: LCC PZ7.C36665 Sc 2023 (print) | LCC PZ7.C36665 (ebook) | DDC 813.6 [Fic]—dc23/eng/20220614
LC record available at https://lccn.loc.gov/2022028281
LC ebook record available at https://lccn.loc.gov/2022028282

10 9 8 7 6 5 4 3 2 1   23 24 25 26 27

Printed in Italy   183
First edition, March 2023
Book design by Maeve Norton

For Jesse, Matthew, and Gillian

How Pangu Created the World

Before the world was the world, the entire universe was stuck inside a single gigantic egg. For thousands of years, the insides of this egg got all mixed up together. Really, this egg was quite the mess, full of confusion and disorder, where very little made sense. Eventually, though, order came along. The universe began to sort itself out so that everything was in balance. And inside the egg, a divine being named Pangu started to form.

He soon grew tired of being inside this one egg, huge as it was—he wanted out!—so he stretched and stretched, twisting and pushing, until even more thousands of years later, the egg finally burst open.

Pangu fell out and his body slowly began to transform. His eyes formed the sun and the moon, his hair the stars. His blood became rivers, his bones mountains, and his skin the soil. His breath shaped into clouds and the echoes of his thoughts formed into thunder. The fur that kept him warm grew into forests; when he got hot, his sweat turned into rain. Tiny insects crawled onto his body and soon became the first humans to walk the earth.

This is the myth of how Pangu created the world.

And how, before there was Order, it was Chaos that ruled . . .

ONE

The entire class goes wild on their instruments at the sound of the school bell. It's become a regular thing at the end of Friday's last class, and for about ten seconds, you've never heard a school band sound so off-key.

Mrs. Battiste finally claps her hands for quiet.

"All right," she calls out over the still-noisy classroom. "Only one week until Spring Revival! Let's try really hard to fit in some extra practice time this weekend. If you've already sold all your raffle tickets for the concert, make sure to turn in your stubs to the office. See everyone on Monday!"

As Libby Pearson (my best friend) puts away her violin beside me, she clumsily bangs the instrument against the leg of her chair. Her parents would freak if they knew, since Libby's violin isn't a rental.

I'm way more careful putting away my clarinet. One, because it *is* a rental, and my parents are always worried about the damage fees. Two, because it's a wind instrument, making it easy for mold to start growing inside. If that happens, you're inhaling that mold right into your lungs each time you play. And three, because not only is that bad for any player, it's especially bad if you've got asthma. Like me.

My asthma is also why I started playing clarinet. "To help build up your lung power," Dr. Park said when she suggested the idea to my parents. "Let's get you some super lungs, Astrid!"

That's me. Twelve-year-old seventh grader Astrid Xu. Star clarinet player at Quincy Elementary School.

So, okay, the last part isn't actually true. If I'm the best clarinet player at school, it's because I'm the *only* clarinet in this year's band class. There *would* have been three of us, but Beatrice Myers moved away during the summer and Owen Chabra decided to switch over to trumpet last minute. And since I'm still working on those super lungs, it also means I'm just an okay player, which doesn't bother me at all. Most of the time.

Jasper Choi (my other best friend) walks over, backpack on and saxophone case in hand. "Bear ate my whole booklet of tickets before I could sell any," he tells Libby and me glumly. "I guess my folks are buying the entire two dozen."

For every ticket a student sells, they get their name entered in a school raffle for a brand-new iPad. Every kid at Quincy Elementary—including me—is hoping to win. And Bear is Jasper's golden retriever. He once ate all the buttons off my jacket, and he farts a lot whenever we take him for walks, but otherwise he's a pretty great dog. Jasper's parents are always asking Libby and me if we want to adopt him, but we know they're just kidding. They spoil Bear nearly as much as Jasper does.

"I left my tickets at the restaurant's front counter," Libby says, snapping her violin case shut. "Our regulars bought them all up!"

The Pearsons own and run Butter, one of Vancouver's fanciest and most famous restaurants. Not everything on the menu is made with butter, but everything still somehow tastes rich, which I guess is why eating there is so expensive.

I check my clarinet reed for cracks (there aren't any) and store it away in my reed container (there aren't any spares left inside; I'll have to remember to refill it before next class). I close the flap and grin at Libby and Jasper. "*Three* booklets sold for me."

My parents might not be rich like the Pearsons, and we don't own a house like the Chois. But it turns out living in an apartment complex isn't just great for when I'm in the middle of baking my family-famous apple dumplings and I'm an apple short. It's also a gold mine for customers.

Libby's mouth forms an O of shock. "No way! That's

awesome! Maybe you can sell some more this weekend."

Jasper looks even glummer than before. "At least my folks might have a real chance at a door prize, right? C'mon, let's get out of here."

Libby grabs her backpack from beneath her seat. "Astrid, you ready?"

Ever since the end of winter break, I've been walking partway home with them. We split up at Forty-Ninth Avenue, with Libby and Jasper off toward their places in one direction and me to our apartment in the other. But back in the fall, Mom would drive Marilla and me to school and then pick us up again nearly every day. Libby and Jasper asked me once why she doesn't anymore, and I just told them she got too busy with work.

Which is a lie.

I wipe out my clarinet with a drying cloth. "Sorry, my dad's picking Marilla and me up today."

Dad decided this morning to work from home, which is a sign of how he thinks the weekend's going to go (hint: not great). He's actually been working from home a lot lately, especially these past few weeks. Sometimes I wonder if he's told anyone at his office why he's not there. What would he have said? How do you explain a sickness you can't really see—one that lives deep in your head?

4

"Okay, text us later," Libby says to me.

"Hey, if you two want to come over tomorrow, I bet we can order in pizza for lunch," Jasper adds.

"Sure," Libby says. "We can bring Bear to the dog park, too."

"Um, let me check, okay?" I say. It depends if Mom's still in bed or not.

My friends wave goodbye and take off.

I finish putting away my clarinet, tucking each piece into its place in its velvet-lined case: bell, lower and upper joints, barrel, and mouthpiece. The case is the mini type, and after I zip it up, I slide it right inside my backpack. I'm not rushing or anything, but I also kind of am. Dad's probably already waiting outside, and Marilla, too, impatient in the back seat.

Also . . . what if today's the day everything actually goes back to normal? Since it's Friday, we'll bring home Chinese or Thai and eat while we all watch a movie on Netflix. The way we always do when things are right and Mom is fine.

"You sounded *great* today, Astrid," Mrs. Battiste says at the doorway as we leave the classroom at the same time. "How are you feeling about your solo next week?"

She's holding her teacher's copy of *Studio Ghibli for Kid Musicians*. We're doing a Studio Ghibli beginner's medley for Spring Revival! (the exclamation point is part of its name, by the way). It's a Quincy tradition that the students get to vote on a concert's music theme, so songs like "Hot Cross Buns" and "Frère Jacques" never stand a chance (no offense to them). One concert, the school band did *Star Wars* songs, and for another, it was Top 2000s Hits.

"Pretty good," I tell my band teacher, when my real answer is something closer to *terrified*. My solo for Spring Revival! is during "Path of the Wind" from *My Neighbor Totoro*. I'm pretty sure I'm looking forward to it as much as I look forward to getting a cavity filled.

Dr. Park *did* warn me that playing wasn't actually going to fix my asthma, but that it would help me learn how to control my breathing, which would then make my asthma easier to deal with. She also said it would take time to show improvement. "Baby steps, Astrid! And lots of playing time, okay?"

I thought I could prove Dr. Park wrong about how long it would take. So back during Winter Fest (Quincy's winter holiday concert), I strolled up onstage, sure my solo would be a breeze. The high notes were my kryptonite, but I'd been hitting them nearly every class.

The concert started out great. But the closer it got to my solo, the more I started imagining messing up in front of everyone. And the more I tried not to imagine it, the more I couldn't help it. Panic crept into my chest like little pinching fingers stealing all my air. When I finally played the high notes, nothing came out of my clarinet but a thin and embarrassing wheeze.

Even now I can shut my eyes and remember the feeling of everyone's eyes on me, so heavy that I could barely play another note the rest of the concert. Marilla never makes fun of me for it, either, which is how I know it's bad.

I've been skating along in band class ever since, hiding my playing behind the sound of everyone else's. I skip high notes whenever I can get away with it. It's only when I'm practicing by myself in my room that playing feels nearly fun again.

When Mrs. Battiste said we'd all get solos for Spring Revival!, I planned on faking a stomachache that night. But then Mom started to get sick again. She started to sleep way too much, the house would become oddly quiet, and Marilla and I never knew what to do, so we just argued to try to fill up that strange silence. That's when I decided I would go to the concert, because if I have the chance to be great onstage, how could Mom *not* want to get better enough to come watch?

But now it's nearly Spring Revival! and I still can't play in front of anyone the way I could before the disaster. I guess I'm too scared to try if it means facing just how badly I'm going to blow my solo. Sure, some days go well enough that I can practically picture Mom in the audience, happy again as she hears me play with super lungs. But panic always ends up creeping close once more, making my air race away, so that I'm back at square one. Those days make the stage feel more for magicians than barely-able-to-play kid-clarinetists.

How am I going to figure out in a week how to get better so that I can make Mom better, too?

"Remember," Mrs. Battiste says to me as she steps into the hall, "practice, practice, practice! I'm sure you'll do wonderfully at the concert."

Deciding she must have the shortest memory in the world for a teacher, I make myself smile back. "I'm sure, too."

TWO

I push open Quincy's front doors and stand on the steps. Our car is parked in the school's drop-off/pickup zone.

Dad's waiting in the driver's seat. He's checking his phone that he's clipped to the dash. He's a project manager, and whenever he works from home, he has to be online during business hours.

My younger sister, Marilla, is in the back seat, the top of her head popping up into view. She's ten years old and in fifth grade. We both have the same long black hair, but she keeps hers pulled into a high ponytail for track and field while I leave mine in a low and messy half bun.

She sees me from her window, leans over the back of Dad's seat, and honks the horn. "Hurry up!"

I climb into the back beside Marilla and pull the car door shut. "Hi, hi, thanks for waiting!" I set my backpack at my feet. "Sorry, it was band class and I had to pack up."

"It's totally fine; we barely waited." Dad pulls out of the school lot and onto the road, whistling badly to BTS on the radio. His face in the rearview mirror is carefully cheerful looking. The more he works from home, the better he's gotten at pretending everything's okay.

"It's not fine; we *totally* waited," Marilla grumbles as she slides down in her seat. Her favorite track pants—her Bruce Lee ones, yellow with the black side stripe—are canary bright beneath the spring sun streaming into the car. "And you were *definitely* slow. I would have just walked home with Glynnis if I'd known you were going to take so long."

"I was ten minutes, tops."

"Who takes ten minutes to leave school on a Friday?" Marilla keeps grumbling, mostly to herself by now.

Glynnis is my sister's best friend. Not only does she live in our apartment building, she and Marilla are in the same homeroom *and* they're both on Quincy's track team. Marilla's over at her place a lot, especially on days like today—when it's somehow hard to breathe at home, even though I'm the only one who has asthma.

I should be glad that she's got a place to go where she can talk as much as she wants without having any worries at all. With someone like Glynnis who has a lot in common with her. But once that place was home, and once that person was me.

Through the car window, houses and shops and traffic slide by. Quincy's one of Vancouver's fastest-changing neighborhoods. Mom and Dad say we're lucky we moved into the area when we did, which was when I was a baby and Marilla not even a speck yet, because everything that's being built now is super expensive. A lot of their old favorite shops and restaurants are disappearing. I'm just glad we live close to most of my friends from school and that Banh Go, maker of the best banh mi sandwiches in the world, is still around.

Marilla lifts her foot to kick mine. I'm in sneakers, but she's wearing real runners since she's in track. Not only can she run way faster than me—her track teacher says she's got a natural talent—she's also taller and more outgoing. Libby and Jasper's nickname for her is Marilla Godzilla (which she doesn't even mind; when she heard, she just thanked them) because she demolishes everything in her way. Most people guess that she's the older sister.

"Hey," she says, "guess how I did on my science test."

I quizzed her in the car on the way to school this morning. Science is one of her favorite subjects. "Ninety percent?"

"One hundred!" She grins at me so widely it's like all our recent arguing never happened. Mom used to say we were stuck together with Xu Glue, we were so close. Like how it used to mean letting Marilla sleep in my bed on the nights she missed Mom most. It meant her not telling on me when I pretended to be sick just to stay home from school, thinking that if Mom was busy taking care of me, she'd forget the illness in her head.

"Hey, that's excellent news," Dad says from the front seat. "I think that calls for celebratory Screamers, don't you two?"

"*Yes!*" Marilla shoots forward in her seat. "And extra swirls of ice cream?" Mac's is on the way home, their slushie-soft-serve combos practically iconic.

Dad laughs. "How can we not?"

"You should tell Mom about your test when we get home," I say to Marilla.

"Okay, sure." But her face changes slightly before she picks up her phone and starts typing, ignoring me, and I can tell she won't. She's remembering the strange silence from this morning and avoiding it the way she always does. I don't get why she does this when she's supposed to be the brave one.

Dad's phone chimes. He turns down the radio.

"Sorry, kids, work call. I'll be done by the time we get to Mac's, okay?"

In response, Marilla slumps down even farther in her seat and keeps texting. Glynnis, probably.

I unzip my backpack and take out a small book.

It smells of vanilla, the way very old books can. Its red leatherlike cover has gone as soft as fabric. There are tiny cracks running all across it, like a vein-filled leaf. The title on the front says *A Handbook of Ancient Chinese Myths* in faded gold letters.

I took it this morning from the box on the dining room table. Mom's an appraiser for a chain of collectible shops, and she gets first dibs on any items they decide not to carry. After her coworker Raj dropped off the box before school, I ate breakfast while checking out what Mom wants to keep. There was a little jeweled elephant and a pearl-covered photo frame and a magazine on heritage tulips. But it was the book I couldn't let go of.

Almost everyone already knows about the Greek gods and goddesses. Deities like Zeus (Roman name, Jupiter) and Athena (Minerva) and Poseidon (Neptune) and all the rest.

But my favorite myths are Chinese ones. Growing up, the stories Mom told us all came from Chinese mythology. There's the goddess Nüwa, the Great Mother of humans, who patched up the sky with colored rocks when it got busted. Fuxi was a god and inventor who created things for mortals like coins and cooking and music. Hou Yi was the archer who shot down all the extra suns after too many rose into the sky at once, keeping Earth from burning to a crisp. Then there's Erlang Shen, who has a truth-seeing eye in the middle of his forehead, and who wasn't just an engineer who kept lands from flooding but also the demigod warrior who fights with his triple-pointed spear. There's his loyal dog, Xiaotian, always at his side.

Holding *A Handbook of Ancient Chinese Myths* as my cereal went forgotten and grew soggy, I had wanted more than anything to rush into Mom's room and show her. To open the book and ask her to tell me all over again which myths she'd loved the most as a kid.

Except she wasn't well enough to do that. Everything around her had grown dark, the morning sun shining into her bedroom windows somehow not mattering.

I flipped through the book quickly—it was nearly time to leave for school—and I grinned at seeing myths I knew, like Hou Yi and Erlang. I saw myths I *didn't* know and my grin got even bigger. I noticed how some myths were just a sentence or two, and some were bunches of pages long. In the back of the handbook were some blank pages, as though for a reader to make notes.

Marilla glanced up from her phone (Dad's old one, reprogrammed so it's only good for texts and calls) and just shrugged when I showed her the cover. She hasn't been interested in mythology for a while now.

I slipped the book into my backpack, making room in between my clarinet case and the small medicine pouch that holds my asthma inhalers. (Ever since my asthma got worse a couple of years ago, Dr. Park recommended that I keep them with me just in case.) My plan was to start reading during the drive to school, but then Marilla asked me to quiz her for her science test. Then Dad got in the mood to talk about Spring Revival! ("You must be getting excited about the concert, Astrid! I make a good test audience if you want to give your solo some practice spins this weekend. Is the class playing something from *Princess Mononoke*?") By the time he was done, we were in the school parking lot.

Now, in the car heading home, I finally open the book again.

More of that old-book-vanilla scent. Like time going backward, back to ancient worlds and even more ancient universes (where depression maybe didn't even exist). There's a proper table of contents, and a name from one of the myths pops out at me.

Fusang.

Mom used to tell Marilla and me the myth of Fusang as a bedtime story, even though it's actually a story about the sun.

I find the right page.

The Legend of Fusang

In the East, there's a special and magical tree called Fusang. Some people believe Fusang is an island rather than a tree, and that is fine, too. (A face can have many expressions, but it's still always the same face.) For this myth, just remember that Fusang is how the day begins.

Now, ten ravens lived on Fusang the tree (or island). These ten ravens were brothers, and they were all very close and got along together very well. They each had bright golden feathers, and whenever they spread their wings out wide, their feathers would release enough light and heat to last for hours. Working together, the raven brothers decided to release days for the world. At the end of the night, when it had been dark for long enough, one of the ten brothers would leave Fusang and fly across the sky. The brothers took turns doing this every day, and this is the rising of the sun every morning.

Marilla and I would curl up together to listen, because the ten raven brothers who lived on Fusang were just as close to one another and always got along. We also convinced ourselves of how we felt cold so that as Mom described the ravens' bright golden feathers being able to create heat and light for hours, we would also suddenly grow warm. By the time she reached the part about the brothers taking turns every morning to become the sun and fly across the sky, we'd be curled up around *her*. As though she could fly away, too, if we weren't careful.

At the bottom of "The Legend of Fusang," there's a

note: *See also: "Hou Yi the Great Archer"* (which makes sense, since the stories are definitely related). I flip the pages to it.

Hou Yi the Great Archer

Hou Yi was a mortal, but he still had incredible strength. Though he was very good at most jobs, he was most skilled in archery. Even the gods and goddesses admired Hou Yi and knew they could ask him for help.

After many long years of taking turns being the sun, the ten raven brothers decided they were tired of having to work alone. One morning, all ten brothers flew from their Fusang home at the same time. So, instead of one raven rising in the sky as the sun, all ten suns rose at once. And because the heat that flowed down to the world was too great to bear, many terrible things began to happen. People got sick. Plants and trees began to die. Rivers and lakes and seas started to shrink. The earth's soil dried up and all its crops did as well.

Hou Yi knew he had to save the world. He went to the royal palace to ask Emperor Jun, the father of the raven brothers, to remove them from the sky. Emperor Jun saw how his realm was burning up, and so he agreed. He gifted Hou Yi with a special bow and arrow for this task, a weapon only an archer as talented as Hou Yi could wield. Made from the bones of magical tigers and the skins of enchanted snakes, it was the one bow and arrow that had the power to reach the sky.

Accepting this gift, Hou Yi proceeded to use this special bow and arrow to shoot down the golden ravens. Nine fell, and as they fell, they turned black, and that is why we have crows on Earth today. As for the tenth, he was allowed to stay in the sky, and he remains there still, the sun that marks a new day.

I start flipping back to the table of contents when a page falls out of the book.

Hoping it didn't fall out because of me, I pick it up, trying to see where in the handbook it belongs. But there are no page numbers, and the words printed on it are too faint to make out. The paper is also oddly thick compared with the other pages of the book, and I wonder if it's actually from something else and just got stuck here by mistake. I examine it more closely and realize it's a piece of paper all folded up. Along one edge, a thin disk of white wax holds it shut. It's super old-looking. Ancient, almost.

I wonder if Mom would care if I cracked the wax open to see what's in—

"We're here!" Dad says cheerfully when his work call ends and he turns into Mac's parking lot.

Marilla whoops. I slip the loose page back into the book and slide both into my backpack.

Dad parks and turns off the engine. But instead of getting out right away, he stays in his seat.

"By the way, Mom has an appointment with Dr. Gale next week." He doesn't know I can see his expression in the rearview mirror and how he's no longer pretending everything is okay. "I know you girls are worried, but you really don't need to be, all right? Mom's going to be fine."

Except that he said this the last time she was sick. And the time before that. I've lost count of how often he's said this.

"Will Mom be okay enough to come see me play?" I make myself ask.

Mom has never missed any of our school events, even if we're just showing people to their seats or helping with stage lights. Before she used to go to all of Marilla's track events, Mom went to sport meets just because Marilla was supervising the little kids' races.

My throat hurts. I've been counting on her coming to Spring Revival! Dad having to come alone—it would feel like something's changed forever. Something you can't take back.

"I know she really doesn't want to miss it," he assures me.

"She'll be better by then, right?" I press.

Dad pauses, then turns to smile at me. He thinks the smile looks stronger than it does.

"Going to see Dr. Gale will help."

THREE

Once we're home, Dad gets back to the work nook and his laptop. Marilla disappears into our shared room upstairs, Screamer in hand.

I go to recycle my empty cup. The kitchen's also empty. Mom's not there, home from work and asking me if I want a snack or how band practice went. Everyone's back now, but the apartment feels as weird as it did this morning. As though our place has become someone's dollhouse and everything's arranged all wrong.

I grab *A Handbook of Ancient Chinese Myths* from my backpack, set the bag on the floor of the front room, and head down the hall.

The walls here are covered with silk paintings. Their glass fronts shimmer with my footsteps as I walk past, so the worlds inside look nearly alive. Mom inherited these paintings from Grandma, who got them from *her* mom. When I was younger, each time I asked, Mom would tell me again about the Chinese myths woven into each painting. She'd be tireless about it, as tireless as she is telling me to keep working on growing super lungs. I would trace the silk threads behind the glass with my fingers, listening and learning and believing everything to be true.

"That's the garden of immortal peaches, Astrid," she would tell me. "There on Kunlun Mountain. It's watched over by Xiwangmu, Queen Mother of the West. To be gifted one of her peaches meant living forever."

"And this painting, Mom?" I would ask.

"The group of Eight Immortals who traveled the lands of ancient China by floating around on clouds. Once they had all been plain old mortals, but because they were good and kind to others, they were granted eternal life."

"What are their names again?"

"That's Han Xiangzi, who always carried his beloved flute. Then Zhang Guolao, whose mini paper donkey in his pocket became a real life-sized one whenever he unfolded it. There's Lu Dongbin, whose sword turned him invisible whenever he wanted. Next is Li Tieguai, who used an iron crutch and always carried around his medicine-filled gourd. Then it's Quan Zhongli, who could bring the dead back to life with a wave of his fan. There's Cao Guojiu, whose jade imperial tablet could purify anything. Then it's He Xiangu—the only female immortal of the group—holding a lotus flower. And, finally, there's Lan Caihe, who some said was a boy and some said was a girl, but who most said was both, and who's the closest to being your age since they're a teenager. Their straw basket was always full of magical herbs and flowers, and their jade clappers made enchanting music. Wouldn't it have been wonderful to hear, Astrid?"

One day Mom's paintings will be Marilla's and mine. Their myths will be ours to tell to others. Not that I can ever tell them the same way. Mom makes them real in my mind even as I know they're only stories.

She does way too many things that only she can.

It's why I just can't let Mom's sickness—how it swallows up all her emotions so she's numb, changes her eyes so they say nothing at all—swallow *her* up, too, so that the solidness of her disappears entirely.

After these paintings, it's framed photos that cover the walls.

Most of them are of Marilla and me, school portraits full of missing teeth and crooked bangs. But there are also photos of us with Mom and Dad from vacations and celebrations. Seeing their wide-open smiles—*real* smiles, back before Mom's depression started getting bad—makes my chest go tight, like it's being squeezed. It actually feels a lot like the pinched breathlessness that crept into me during Winter Fest, my panic a cold trickling river.

One of the photos on the wall is of Grandpa. Mom's

dad. I never met him since he died of a heart attack before I was born. But Mom and Dad said he had depression, too. His own fog that came and went.

Fog is how one of Mom's first doctors described her depression to us. That it makes it hard for her to see the world through it, and how when the fog is especially thick and stubborn, it becomes even harder for Mom to remember to keep looking. How it can almost trick her into believing there's not much beyond that fog at all.

Mom's gotten new doctors since then and changed medications, too. But the fog always comes back. The same way real fog sometimes does even after the sun's burned it away.

The doctors say some of Grandpa's fog likely passed down to Mom and that's why she gets sick now, too. Not that it's the only reason why. Dad says depression is kind of like a weed aboveground, and how beneath, its roots can come from all sorts of directions.

For a few seconds, I just stand outside my parents' door. I wonder if I should make Marilla come with me to see how Mom's doing. Xu Glue sisters. "Better together," Mom used to say.

But Marilla's already busy talking to Glynnis. She's going over there any minute because the Millers just got Disney+.

I knock.

"Mom?" I whisper loudly into the crack where the door meets the frame. "It's Astrid." I push the door open.

The drapes are pulled. The spring sun that turned Marilla's yellow track pants canary bright loses power in here, and I blink in the light that lies and says it's still winter.

Mom's a lump in bed; she hasn't gotten up all day, telling me just how thick the fog is. It's spilling out of her head and twisting into the room, an invisible snake that says she doesn't want us here (even if she's never, ever said that before). It's this snake of fog that always manages to chase away Marilla. When she says to me that Mom's not visible anymore.

"Astrid." Mom's voice is tired even though she's been sleeping so much. "You okay?"

I move closer. "Hi, Mom. Raj from work dropped off some stuff for you this morning. There's the mythology book you picked out—do you want to see it?"

"Not right now."

Beneath the covers, Mom doesn't move, and the pinched feeling in my chest screws up even more. I think of my rescue inhaler and wonder if I might need it.

I grip the mythology book tighter. It's supposed to do the trick. She's supposed to sit up and say, "Myths? How can I say no? Now pull the drapes so we can read it!"

Before she can tell me she's too tired to listen, I sit down on the bed beside her. "Listen, I'll read you a myth, okay?"

"Astrid—"

"It's Shennong's." Before she can stop me, I open the book and start reading the famous Chinese doctor's story out loud:

Shennong the Medicine King

Also known as the Medicine King, Shennong is one of the oldest gods in Chinese mythology. The middle of his body was clear as a crystal, which helped him to see what happened to his food as he ate. This was how he was able to declare which foods would help mortals stay the most healthful.

After people in his village kept growing ill, he decided to find out the cause. He wandered all the local forests and climbed all the nearby mountains. He tested plants by eating them and observing their effect on his body. If a plant passed through his stomach gently, he called it a medicine. But if it hurt him, he called it a poison, and he invented tea to drink to help him wash such poisons from his stomach.

In time, he discovered which foods made people ill, and his entire village was cured. Soon he traveled the world to pass on his knowledge. He shared all his notes with Earth's earliest humans, teaching them which foods were best and which poisons were worst. He showed mortals how to farm and how to grow plants and how to stay healthy. One day, the Medicine King tested a food that turned out to be a very bad poison, the worst he'd ever had. He drank his tea quickly but not quickly enough. As he watched the poison cling to his stomach, Shennong died, wondering how he would pass on this last bit of knowledge.

I reach the end and stop reading. "Want another?" I ask, knowing she doesn't.

She shuts her eyes for a long minute before opening them again. "Soon. I promise. We'll read it together."

Mom's really good with promises. But not the ones she makes when she's sick.

I close the book. "When, do you think?"

Mom sits up against the headboard. She looks like Mom but also not. Like dust coated over something brighter. "Come here for a second."

I flop down onto her lap, squeezing her as though I could squeeze her sickness away so only Mom is left. She squeezes me back, but there's a tiredness to her arms. I remember the doctors saying how strong the fog can be.

"One day I *will* be better," she says. "I wish I could tell you when, but I can't. Just believe me for now, all right?"

I nod, even though believing isn't as easy as it sounds. If it were, Mom would already be better. I'd have super lungs and wouldn't be worried about Spring Revival! at all.

I'll keep trying to believe you'll be saved, Mom.

But it doesn't mean I'm going to stop looking for a way to do it myself.

FOUR

Our poster of the Kitchen God is next to the fridge. "His favored language is food," Grandma said when she taped it to the wall. "And where food comes together is where your voices will be clearest. He'll watch over this home, making sure everyone will stay healthy. Think of sweet things and he'll bring sweetness back."

We used to leave offerings for the Kitchen God only at Chinese New Year. It was little more than a game. The Kitchen God was especially careful to listen then, and Marilla and I would pile mandarins and almond cookies on the small plate. "Dear Kitchen God," we would say out loud together. "Here are some sweet things to remind you to tell the Jade Emperor how we've all been good this year."

New Year was also when Mom would tell us the story of the nian, which is in the handbook, too.

The Myth of the Nian

Beneath the very oldest mountains of China, there once lived monsters called nian. They had the bodies of powerful bulls, necks and heads of great dragons, with a giant pointed horn on top for attacking prey. They ate crops and animals, and when those were scarce, hunted humans who had strayed too far from the nearby village.

But then winters would come. Crops slept, animals stayed in barns, and humans kept warm in their homes. On the eve of one new year, when the nian couldn't bear their hunger any longer, they thundered free of their mountain and charged straight into the village. They ate all they could find, from stored crops to whole families. They especially enjoyed eating the children.

This went on for many years. Every night before the new year, the villagers carefully locked all their food away and hid in the dark. But still the nian came.

One winter, a visitor came by. Since he had saved his own village from the nian, the visitor knew what to do to drive the monsters away. On New Year's Eve he told the villagers to hang darkened lanterns in front of all their homes. He had everyone wear robes of red cloth and lion masks, for nian were afraid of the golden beasts. In the center of the village, he set out a bed of burning coals.

At midnight, the earth shook and trembled with the arrival of the nian. But when all the houses' lanterns turned on at once, the creatures went still, frightened by the bright light. Villagers swirled their robes and the nian fell back from their redness; the villagers showed their lion masks and the nian turned away. The village fed dried bamboo stalks to the burning coals and the stalks burst apart, whistling and snapping. And as the air filled with noise, the nian rushed out of the village, never to return.

Nowadays, Chinese New Year celebrations have lion dances, which represent how the villagers successfully chased the nian away. We hang up red streamers instead of wearing red robes, set off firecrackers for the noise, and send fireworks in the sky to symbolize the bright lights. And just as Marilla and I got older—and we started noticing more when Mom was sick—our offerings to the Kitchen God also began to change. We started bribing the Kitchen God even when it wasn't New Year. Wishing.

Kitchen God, here's some Smarties, please make Mom better.

The last chocolate eggs from our Easter baskets.

A White Rabbit Candy.

But now Marilla says it's just a waste of food and how we're silly to believe. It's the same way she purposely picks the number four as her favorite, when we both know it's actually the worst number of all (because it sounds like *dead* in Chinese). I think the Kitchen God ignoring us is why she's not into mythology anymore.

"You know all of that isn't real, right, Astrid?" she once said to me. "If it was, nothing would ever be wrong here, and that's just not true."

All I know is that I'm the only one still leaving offerings to the Kitchen God. And wishing for Mom to get better doesn't feel like just a game anymore.

I drag the step stool to the front of the fridge and climb up. The small ceramic plate on top is still there. And the food that I put on it a couple weeks ago—the slice of dried mango, chunk of rock sugar, and Fruit Crème cookie—is dusty.

"You're not serious, are you? Talking to the Kitchen God *again*?"

I glance down as Marilla steps into the kitchen, holding her emptied Screamer cup.

The tips of my ears grow warm at the laugh in her voice. I don't look at her when I answer, instead just pick up the plate from the top of the fridge. "I'm definitely serious. Do you want to help?"

"No thanks, I'm busy." She tosses the cup into the garbage and leaves. "Don't use the last of the Oreos!"

Like texting Glynnis all day long is actually being busy, I think, deciding not to let Marilla's attitude bother me. I carry the plate down and throw the old food away. From my jeans pocket I take out the bag of Skittles that Dad let me buy at Mac's and pour a bunch onto the plate. I stare hard at the candy and start.

Dear Kitchen God. It's Astrid Xu again, of apartment 24 at

1996 Linden Street in Vancouver. *Sorry that my sister's not here again—I think she's had a hard time believing in you ever since Mom got sick. I'm leaving you some Skittles now just in case you're going to make a report to the Jade Emperor soon. I know Grandma says it's not about just offering you sweets to prove we deserve to be blessed, but how it's also about us having good thoughts. Which means the Jade Emperor needs to know that I'm going to find a way to save Mom. She'll be able to get out of bed and go back to the way she says she most likes to be. So, if you can pass this on and maybe send some luck my way, I would appreciate it a lot. Thank you.*

I pour out a few more Skittles because I figure it can't hurt. I put the plate back on top of the fridge, pick up my bag, and go to my room.

Marilla's at her desk, taking stuff out from her backpack now that it's the weekend. Her half of the room is as messy as always, with books and magazines on her bed and clothes at her feet. Her treasured Bruce Lee poster hangs on her wall. His most famous movie line—*Be like water*—fills one of the two oversized speech bubbles next to his head. In the other bubble is *KIYAAAH!!!* (Bruce Lee is also famous for doing a lot of yelling when he fought.)

The kung fu legend watches as I toss my bag onto my bed. I plonk down on top of my covers. "When are you going to Glynnis's?"

Marilla shrugs, still poking around in her bag. "Actually, her sisters are taking her out." .

"Oh. Sorry about that." I feel bad but not *that* bad. I don't like the weird quiet, either, but with Marilla around, at least it's not so loud (even if we do argue a lot of the time). "Well, we can just hang out here. Dad's done with work in, like, an hour. And it's Friday, so it's takeout and movie night."

"I guess." She sounds bored.

"You should go tell Mom about your science test, by the way. Even if she's sleeping, I bet she won't mind."

"Yeah, okay, I will," she says, not getting up.

You're Marilla Godzilla! I think. *You're not supposed to be scared!*

From the wall, Bruce Lee's still watching me. I look at his speech bubble again.

Be like water.

It means to go with the flow. To work with things that get in your way instead of fighting them because that's actually the easiest path toward your goals. And how being okay with the things you can't change is important for happiness since balance in life is key to that happiness.

I guess Bruce Lee could have just said *that*. But I like how he used water to show what he meant. Because just like how he was a master of kung fu, water is a master of adapting, becoming soft enough to wiggle between your fingers or hard enough that it can smash through rock. If you learn to "be like water," you don't freak out when something doesn't go exactly as planned, since you'll have already figured out that flowing around the rock of your mess-up is way easier and faster than trying to break through it.

Dr. Park didn't know that by suggesting the clarinet—for helping when my inhaler doesn't work or when panic can lead to an asthma attack—she was trying to help me be like water.

Marilla and I also try to be like water when it comes to Mom being sick, but it's harder than it seems, so we're still not getting it right. For Marilla, it means never talking about it; for me, I just want to smash apart the rock that I picture as Mom's depression. Now, whenever I bug Marilla to help me think of ways we can help Mom, ways that doctors and medicines don't know about yet, Marilla just flows far away from me.

Not surprisingly, Marilla still hasn't gotten up from her desk, so I take out *A Handbook of Ancient Chinese Myths* from my backpack. I'm bummed that I probably won't be going to Jasper's tomorrow, not with Mom being so sick, but at least now I have the whole weekend to read. Plus practice my clarinet.

My sister twists in her seat to face me. "You're still reading that old book?" Her expression says she's annoyed. "You already know all the stories."

I remind myself to *be like water* and not argue. So instead of telling her she doesn't have to *hate* mythology—same as how she doesn't have to be scared of talking to Mom—I just say, "There's still tons of myths we don't know. You can read with me if you want."

She snorts. "They're stories for kids. Same as how wishing to the Kitchen God is also for kids." She picks up her phone and I hear her start texting.

An ugly prickling feeling runs through me at the idea of Marilla and Glynnis laughing about me—*when I'm just trying to help Mom!*—and I flip open the handbook, determined to show how I don't care what either of them thinks.

"At least I'm doing *something*," I mutter extra loudly on purpose.

"Talking to a god that doesn't even exist isn't doing anything at all. You should grow up, Astrid."

My cheeks grow warm the same way my ears did back in the kitchen. "Then why do you still make wishes when you blow out your birthday candles? I've *seen* you." I stick my face back into the book. "Just go back to texting your BFF, why don't you?"

Marilla sets her phone down and walks over. She's got

that look on her face, her Marilla Godzilla look, and I move the book out of her reach, suddenly worried about what I've started.

"It's my turn with it," she says, trying to grab the book. "I'll show you the real baby parts."

"Shut up." I wave it up high, and the folded-up piece of paper from earlier falls out onto my lap.

"What's that?" Marilla reaches for it.

I grab it first. "It's just a part of the book. Go away."

"It's not even your book, it's *Mom's.*" She tugs at the paper, her face going red. "I get to look at it, too!"

A wave of anger washes over me. *Now* she wants to talk about Mom? I tug back, harder, and Marilla finally lets go.

In my hand, the wax seal cracks open.

SNAP!

The breaking sound is louder than I expected. Like it's not just wax I've broken but something heavier, more important—something that maybe wasn't meant to be broken at all. No longer stuck together, the piece of paper instantly unfurls into a loose scroll. There's the feeling of a small cool wind right against my fingers.

Marilla steps back. "What's that?"

"Um, a scroll?"

Too curious to stay mad (the same goes for me), she sits down on my bed. "*That* came from the mythology book?"

"It did, but I think it's from something else and just got stuck inside for a long time." I start unrolling the scroll. There are three small line drawings along the top, the way old-fashioned books sometimes have art at the edges of their pages.

A bird's wing.

A bird's head.

A feather.

Having no idea what the drawings mean, I unroll the scroll all the way. It's about the size of the paper Dad uses in the printer. It's also super old-feeling, almost like the tissue paper you use for gift bags but even softer. And it's more yellow than white, another sign it's old.

"It looks like it should be in a museum or something," Marilla says.

"Right? Hey, this is Chinese writing." I stare at the black characters written on the scroll. The faint writing that I noticed earlier was the backside of the paper, and though the ink on the front is also faded, it's still really easy to tell that it's not the English alphabet. "Too bad neither of us can read Chinese." Dad can, but he's working. And Mom can, too, but . . .

"Oh, I've got a translation app on my phone!" Marilla grabs her phone from her desk and plops back down beside me. She opens up the app and holds it over the scroll, waiting as it scans the characters.

"You know those translation apps aren't very good," I say as her screen blinks, the characters changing over into letters. I remember testing one once on a Chinese take-out menu and laughing at all the mistakes.

"Still better than nothing. And this app is supposed to be good at catching key words."

The screen finishes flashing and we read it together:

This is the Scroll of Chaos, which speaks of a woken demon and a terrible flood that ends the realm. You who unsealed the scroll and set the demon free have set this prophecy into motion. You are the only one who can now stop it. Your hope waits at the top of Kunlun Mountain, home of the gods and goddesses, in the trees of Fuxi and the phoenix. There your one chance will be found.

Chaos? Prophecy? Kunlun Mountain?

A shiver runs through me, even as I tell myself there's no way any of this can be real. As much as I want to believe in myths like Kunlun Mountain and Fuxi, they're just that—nothing but stories and silk paintings behind glass. Because otherwise, the Kitchen God would have heard me by now . . . right?

"Huh," Marilla mutters. "*Weird*. Soooo . . . what's with this 'Scroll of Chaos'?"

"It's supposed to be this right here." I point at the paper. "And I'm the person who just unsealed it."

My sister exits the app on her phone and the translation disappears from the screen. "It's obviously a part of the book. Just another myth."

I nod. This makes the most sense. Being powerful enough to bring a myth to life would be amazing, but not *this* kind of myth. Save a realm full of gods and goddesses? I can barely play clarinet!

The walls of the bedroom begin to shake. The blind over the window rattles. The floor dips and something rolls off Marilla's desk with a thump.

"Uh-oh," she whispers when everything goes still again. "Was that an earthquake?"

Vancouver is overdue for the next Big One, but everyone's been saying that for years. And this one was small. "It's okay, it's already over."

"And now my phone isn't working. Look—the clock's frozen." Marilla shakes her phone, then holds it out so I can see how the second hand (she chose the analog display) is jiggling back and forth in place on the screen, trying to move. It says time is stuck halfway between a minute ago and now.

"Dad probably just needs to reset—" I stop, the rest of my words drying up. Because in my hand, the scroll is . . . changing. *Growing.* It's no longer as big as a sheet of printer paper but two sheets put together. I blink, and now it's as big as the *Vancouver Sun* that Dad still gets delivered every

Saturday, the newspaper so oversized he folds it up in order to read.

I drop the scroll onto my bed as though it's on fire. My lungs gather up tight, like someone's got a fist around them. For a wild second I'm sure the earthquake actually *was* the Big One, and that I've been knocked out so all this is a dream. None of this can be real.

The scroll keeps growing. Now it's as huge as Mom's favorite beach blanket. It covers up both our legs, the far end of it hanging off the edge of my bed.

I shake my head. "Nope, not happening," I say out loud. *Wake up, Astrid, wake up!*

"Whatever this is, it's *definitely* happening." Marilla's eyes are huge as she stares at the still-growing scroll. "What do we do?"

"I don't know." If this is real, could it mean the *prophecy* is real, too? And that I'm supposed to *save an entire realm*? Impossible. *No way.*

I grab Marilla's hand and yank us back toward the wall, trying to get as far away from the scroll as we can. Away from everything it means. Panic fills up my chest so I'm running out of room to breathe, just like we have no more room to move.

The scroll slides off the bed. It tilts itself upright so it's standing on the floor.

I wait for it to grow even bigger. But it doesn't. It just stays there, a door-sized piece of paper standing up in the middle of our room. It actually *looks* like a door.

"I think it's done growing," Marilla says. She stands up on the bed, and I wonder if she's going to try one of her Bruce Lee kicks on the door. *Kiyaaah!*

I try to take slow, deep breaths, fighting the panic that won't fully leave. Because I'm not sure it's over yet—not if the prophecy is actually real. "I think . . . I think I'm supposed to go through it."

Marilla stares down at me. "Are you *serious?*"

"Because I'm the one who broke the seal."

"It's just a myth! Prophecies aren't real."

"I'm not saying I want to go, I'm just *saying*," I sputter. "I mean, that door looks pretty real to me!"

"So what?!" She falls back down on the bed and grabs my hand. "Dad! Mom! HELP!"

But before I can add anything else, the entire room starts tilting. The door swings inward as it becomes a hole in the floor.

Through the doorway I see nothing but darkness.

"Aaaah!" Gravity tosses me off the bed and sends me flying through the air—straight toward the doorway.

And Marilla, still holding my hand, comes right along with me.

FIVE

We tumble through the doorway. At the last second, I fling back my hand to grab the door frame, but it actually bends away from me. Nowhere to go now but into the darkness.

The bedroom disappears and we keep falling, faster and faster. The walls and the floor and all the furniture disappear from around us and I can't see anything at all. Air rushes past in whooshes and whistles. At one point I realize my hand is empty—Marilla's let go! I try to call her name, but I can't catch my breath. Fear drums inside my throat—where are we going? What is this?! I'm still falling and I have no clue how that's possible. (Then again, nothing that's happened seems possible. But here we are, nose-diving through a hole that opened up in our bedroom floor.)

That's because this is all a dream, Astrid! I yell at myself. *You did hit your head during the earthquake, just as you first thought. Soon you'll wake up and you can go check on Mom and Dad and Marilla. It'll all be okay.*

Right, then. I keep falling, but now that I know I'm just dreaming, I simply wait to see what happens next.

"Ouch!" I land hard and mostly on my butt. Rubbing the pain away, I slowly sit up and look around the dream world.

The first thing I notice is that the darkness from the doorway is because it's nighttime here. Dreaming has sped up time.

The second is the blanket of stars overhead. I've never seen stars so bright before, not even far outside the city where there's no light pollution. Here, they're splatters of silver paint spilled onto black, all glittery and flashing.

Next, I notice the ground my hands are digging into. I'm sitting in a huge field of grass, blades grown so tall they'll be at my knees once I stand up (or maybe even higher). Farther out, trees surround the field in a ring of thick black shadows.

An odd, tingling feeling crawls over my scalp as I spin in a slow circle and look all around.

Why does this dream feel so *real*? The stars are so bright they hurt my eyes, actually making them water, and since when can dreams do that? I sniff my hand, and the scent of grass is so strong it makes my eyes water some more. A night wind rustles the field and it lifts goose bumps on my arms. I yank up the sleeve of my thin sweater and run a finger along the bumps. I feel each and every one as clearly as if I were awake.

The pit of my stomach bottoms out and I feel dizzy. Abruptly, I fall back into the grass and lie down. Ignoring my pounding heart, I shut my eyes, willing myself to slip from the dream (this *has* to be a dream!) and back into a bonked-my-head kind of sleep. After that, I'll wake up for good and everything will be just the way it was. (Right? Right!)

Something touches my shoulder.

It's just the grass, I think, trying to be sleepy. *So tall that it's brushing against me.*

It happens again.

I crack open an eye.

A small black cat is at my side. Fur darker than night, eyes glowing bright canary yellow. Its paw is on my shoulder and its huge eyes stare down at me.

"Hi, dream cat," I whisper. "I'm going to sleep now, okay?"

"Astrid!" its little mouth shrieks. "It's me, Marilla!"

"Aaah!" I sit upright and instantly try to back away. My breaths come in fast little whistles. "What did you just say? Did you just *talk*?"

The cat follows along. It bats my shoulder with its paw again. "Stop! It's me, Marilla!"

I utter a high-pitched scream. "This isn't happening, this isn't happening, this isn't—"

"It is! We fell through the doorway in the floor of our bedroom and now we're in this field."

I stop moving. "What—how—*why*? You're a *cat*?"

"Like I have any idea what's going on! How do I change back? Why are *you* still human? *And where the heck are we?*"

I can't deal with Marilla's voice coming out of a cat. I shake my head, trying to clear it. "Okay, listen, we must have *both* hit our heads during the earthquake and this is all just a shared dream."

"This can't be a dream if this hurts." She swipes at my leg through my jeans. "It hurts, right?"

Her cat claws are super sharp. "Ow!"

"See? So what's going on?"

I bend down and touch the grass again. The blades feel as real as ever. *Way too real for a dream.* "I have no clue. I think you're right that we're wide-awake, though." I look up at the painfully bright stars and a cold knot grows in my gut—what *is* going on?

Something lands on the grass beside me. *Thump.*

I reach out and feel around in the grass. "My backpack!" I tell Marilla as I pick it up. "It must have fallen through the doorway after us."

Another *thump*. This time it's *A Handbook of Ancient Chinese Myths* that's lying on the ground.

"Look!" Marilla paws at something nearby. It's her

Bruce Lee track pants and the sweatshirt she was wearing today; next to them is her phone. "They must have come off me on my way through the door. And my phone was in my hand."

I stuff all of it into my backpack. I also make sure that my clarinet case—which has been inside my bag this whole time—didn't get cracked in the fall, and it seems fine (which is good, because Mom and Dad would kill me).

"Astrid, what if the earthquake wasn't an earthquake?" In the dark, the yellow of Marilla's cat eyes glows like lamps. The fur along her back is all raised. "What if it was actually some kind of secret government project and we're stuck inside an experiment? What if this isn't even Earth? What about *aliens*?"

Marilla panicking makes *my* panic want to explode, for my asthma to take over. But that wouldn't help either of us right now. I'm *the older sister*, I remind myself, no matter how many people might guess it's Marilla—I've got to stay calm. I almost want to ask her how she can believe in secret human experiments and aliens if she doesn't believe in myths, but I don't. We'd only argue again.

"Look, we just need to find the scroll," I say, trying to sound confident. I slip my backpack on. "Once we do, we can figure out how to change it back into a door and then we can go home." A part of me would be perfectly happy never seeing the scroll again, but since it got us here, I bet we also need it to get back. "We'll be back in time for dinner, even."

We search together for the printer-sized piece of paper and, a minute later, we find it in the grass not too far away. Since the doorway's disappeared, the scroll must have shrunken back to its normal size. The tissue-like paper is bent all over but not ripped.

"Okay, now what?" Marilla asks as I pick it up.

I haven't thought this far ahead. "Maybe we need to break the seal again? That's the only thing I did to the scroll before it changed."

"You can't break it again if it's already broken."

"Well, the two halves are still stuck on it . . ."

"Wouldn't that be more like . . . *crumbling* it?"

"Let's just try. If it doesn't work, I'll think of something else."

"Like what?"

"I don't know. *Something*, okay?"

My sister sighs super loudly. "Why'd you have to break that seal in the first place, anyway? Maybe we wouldn't be here if you'd been more careful."

I nearly sputter at how unfair she's being. "I wouldn't have broken it if you hadn't been trying to take it from me!"

"I was just trying to look at it with you!"

"Whatever, no you weren't—"

"Wait." Marilla's ears slant back and forth the way a real cat's do when it's listening carefully. "Do you hear that?" She turns to face the trees behind me, her paws silent on the grass.

"I don't hear anything." But I turn to look with her, and as bright as the stars are overhead, they light up the sky more than show what's in the woods, so the trees are still just black shadows. "Maybe it's just a wild animal. If it shows up, we can hide in the grass until it goes away."

"It's not an animal, it's the trees. Something's moving through them."

As soon as she says this, I hear it, too. The sound of thousands of leaves being shaken like there's a windstorm. I'm about to say just that—*It's only the wind*—when the noise grows louder. So that now it's a wind that's *roaring*.

A menacing feeling comes over me, like I'm walking past a house and there's a snarling dog right behind the fence, watching me as I go.

A great shadow forms above the trees. Against the star-lit sky, it looks like a low cloud gathering itself. Maybe it *is* just a storm.

Marilla leaps onto my legs and climbs all the way up into my arms. Whiskers trembling, she stares at the cloud as do I. "Whatever that is, it's headed this way."

She's right. The shadow cloud is moving toward us. But instead of drifting gently or floating its way over, it's like a plane zigzagging wildly through the air. As it flies over the woods, the trees beneath it go white and ghostly looking, either dried up, frozen, or just plain dead, I don't know. But the shadow cloud must be leaving something super bad in its wake. And Marilla and I are right in its path.

I hurriedly roll up the scroll and stuff it into my jeans pocket. I grip my cat sister tight, spin around, and start running.

"Where are we going?" Marilla yells. Her claws dig into the sleeves of my shirt.

"Somewhere else!" Grass pushes against my legs as I swerve right, trying to beat the shadow cloud's speed. It's swooping all over the place, but it's still mainly heading out toward the field and away from the trees. Right before it can cross over us, we'll dodge and race back to where it came from.

The roaring sound grows louder. I keep running, my asthma already starting up. I try not to think about my rescue inhaler that's in my backpack, the one I can't reach and that Dr. Park says I'm supposed to use if I ever can't catch my breath (which is basically right now). My heart pounds so hard I can feel it echo along to my wrists. I dare a peek over my shoulder. The shadow cloud is just behind us and swerving in our direction.

I veer left. *Gotta get out of its way!*

It keeps coming, darting its way closer. Blades of grass beneath it instantly stop swaying and go pale. The odd lack of color sticks out in the darkness, nearly as bright as the stars.

"No, go right!" Marilla screams.

"I . . . did!" I puff out. My lungs are burning. I'm still running but definitely more slowly now. "It changed course!"

"It changed back!"

I charge right, aiming straight for the trees now. I don't *think* it's actually following us—its goal has to be something more important—but I can't be sure. Otherwise, I might just chance hiding. It would be safer than needing to run. Than needing to be strong.

I stumble hard over the grass.

My grip automatically tightens as I fall forward, knowing I can't stop, and Marilla's yowl is exactly like a cat's.

Before I can meet the ground with my face, a hand on my arm pulls me back to my feet.

"Are you able to keep running?" a deep voice asks me from the dark.

My "Who's asking?" turns into a long and wimpy wheeze, and the next thing I know, Marilla and I are being tossed onto someone's back.

He (whoever "he" is) starts running across the field, piggybacking us. He's so fast I hold on tighter, sure I'm going to slip off. Squished into a ball of fur in my arms, my sister yowls again. She sticks out her paws and starts trying to swipe at the stranger.

"Put the claws away," the voice growls. "I'm trying to get us all to safety."

It's true. Over his shoulder I see the same trees I was running toward, way closer now.

A shape lopes up alongside the stranger. It's a dog, about the size of Bear but more like a greyhound than a retriever. That's about all I can tell before it takes off through the grass.

More footsteps come up behind us.

"Go right!" whoever it is calls out.

The person piggybacking us turns as directed, still running. I twist my head and see the shadow cloud in the sky finally start to angle away from us. It crosses the rest of the field and disappears over the woods.

When we finally reach the line of trees, the stranger stops running and sets us down on the ground. I back up as fast as I can. I'm still out of breath as I stare up at the three figures, with Marilla shoved under my arm like a plushie. Starlight is broken up as it streams down through the trees keeping the strangers mostly hidden.

"Who are you?" I ask, getting to my feet, still squishing Marilla in my grip.

The gray dog emerges first. It's wearing armor plates that gleam a dull and darkened gold beneath the silvery light. The plates wrap around its chest and come up over the back of its head. There's gold plating around its arms and legs, too. It cocks its head at me and meets my stare.

An odd feeling like I know this dog from somewhere tingles up my spine. *I know you, but from where?*

Marilla climbs up onto my shoulder, out of the dog's reach. She hisses.

The dog says, "Astrid Xu of apartment 24 at 1996 Linden Street, Vancouver?"

I take another step back, surprised. Not because a dog is talking to me—I guess I'm really getting used to Marilla as a cat—but because it knows who I am.

One of the other two figures walks over. "Well, then? Are you Astrid Xu?"

It's the same voice that asked the first question, and now I recognize it. It's not the dog at all but whoever piggy-backed us and saved us from the shadow cloud (even if we didn't ask them to).

I'm about to say thank you when the light shifts and I finally get a good look at his face.

He's Chinese. Just like Marilla and me. He's wearing gold armor all over his body, same as the dog. His helmet is made out of even more gold, with a red feathery plume poking out from the top. The red matches the red of his shirt and pants that he's wearing beneath his armor. His long cape is also red, flowing over his back and nearly to the ground.

A bow and arrow hang from his waist.

He's holding a long, triple-pointed spear.

And on his forehead, just peeking out from the edge of his helmet, is the bottom half of a large third eye.

My mouth drops open.

I can think of only one person who carries a triple-pointed spear and has a truth-seeing eye on his forehead: Erlang Shen, mythological China's most powerful warrior!

I stare at the gray dog. It's got to be Xiaotian, the warrior's loyal battle dog, always known to be at his side!

Erlang Shen points his spear at me. "Will my spear make you finally answer?"

"Kiyaaah!" Marilla—aka Bruce Lee, kung fu legend, except cat version—leaps right at Erlang. Claws out.

He yelps as she lands on his head. He drops his famous

spear and it thumps down onto the grass. Starlight flashes off his gold armor as he tries to free himself.

"Don't hurt her!" I yell. "That's my sister!"

Xiaotian circles Erlang's feet and barks up at Marilla.

"Howl, retreat!" the warrior commands with Marilla's paws still wrapped around his head.

Instantly the dog pulls back and sits down.

Howl? Erlang's nicknamed his legendary battle dog *Howl?*

Erlang finally plucks Marilla free and drops her to the grass. His expression is more exasperated than anything. Being a demigod hero and a warrior known for fighting off monsters means you're probably supposed to go easy on helpless animals. Maybe especially once you've been told it's actually a human.

"I'm Astrid Xu," I say. "Are you really Erlang Shen?"

"I am." He slides his spear back into its holder lying across his back, then scowls at Marilla. "We weren't expecting you to arrive with a cat."

"I'm a human and my name is Marilla," she mutters. She crosses her arms, which looks super strange since she's a cat. "Something must have gone wrong after we fell through the doorway."

"But you're not supposed to be real," I say to the warrior, still stunned. "You're a *myth.*"

"A myth in your realm, yes. But here in Zhen—which

you know as mythological China—I promise you I am very real. My uncle, the Jade Emperor, used his power to bring you from your realm to ours."

My head spins. The Jade Emperor? He's basically mythological royalty, having rule over everything! "Why would someone so important want *us* here?"

The shadows behind Erlang shift, and the last figure, the person who told Erlang which way to run, comes to stand in front of us.

"Because it was you who broke the seal of the Scroll of Chaos, Astrid," they say. "Only you can seal it again."

Like Erlang, they're also Chinese. But their black hair is cut short into a bob and their face is younger and softer looking than Erlang's. Their shirt and pants are jade green, and over this they're wearing a long blue silk robe with wide blue-and-gold sleeves that flow past their hands.

A silver hoe rests over one of their shoulders; a straw basket hangs off its end.

"Lan Caihe of the Eight Immortals!" I practically shout. Who else in Chinese mythology is a teenager *and* carries a basket full of magical treasures? I'm so excited at who I'm meeting, I can almost push away how I'm supposed to save a realm I doomed in the first place. *Almost.*

They smile. "You can just call me Sae, short for Caihe. Welcome to Zhen. I'm sorry the first creature you and your sister had to meet was a demon."

I shiver, remembering that feeling of menace. "So that shadow cloud thing is the demon I woke up when I opened the scroll?"

"Yes. The demon is still young, only just beginning. It is stealing energy from the realm by casting a spell on everything in its path and putting it to sleep. We call it grim magic." They gesture to the field behind them, the swaths of grass cutting through it turned ghost white. "It's how the demon will gain power on its way to making the ancient prophecy of flooding the realm come true."

"I really set that prophecy into motion?"

They nod. "One that you now need to stop."

"But I don't know how to save an entire realm." My stomach wobbles. I never imagined that finding out my favorite myths were real would fill me with as much dread as awe. I wonder if admitting how I've already messed up a school concert might get me off the hook.

"We'll help, of course," Sae says. "But in the end, it'll be you who will have to fight the demon."

I nearly choke on my spit. "I have to *fight* him?"

Marilla—who's now made friends with Howl, the immortal dog lying on the grass while my sister walks all over him—peers up. "But Astrid can't fight. She can barely run."

"Gee, thanks," I protest (even though she's not actually wrong, and even though I don't actually want to do this).

Erlang sighs. "We did acknowledge it was unfortunate that it was a mortal who ended up finding and unsealing the scroll. But the realms work as they work and there's no telling where a spin of the universe will land. And so here you are."

"Can't the scroll be wrong?" I ask hopefully. "I mean, our realm even gets basic news wrong all the time."

"It's not wrong," Sae says. "Though the story of the Scroll of Chaos has never become myth in your realm, it has been a part of Zhen's history since the beginning of our time. Everyone in the realm learns it, just as those in your realm know its oldest stories. The prophecy is that once Chaos is reborn upon the breaking of the scroll's seal, he will soon grow strong enough to release a great and terrible flood to destroy the realm forever. And the only person who can stop this from happening will be the same person who broke the seal. Only this person will find the way to beat the demon in battle."

"But how do you know it's even real? Lots of our oldest stories aren't real at all."

"We actually only found physical proof of the scroll

three centuries ago. That was when a group of the emperor's explorers discovered it deeply buried in ancient caves. It was mixed in with other educational papers—on stars, the seas, things like that. But there were also written legends, and when the discovers saw the scroll sealed with white wax, they knew what it was. The emperor decided to keep it hidden deep in the caves, but a century ago, it went missing. We've been searching for it since— not just in Zhen, but everywhere in the universe, including other realms of other worlds. The seal being broken finally revealed where it was and who had broken it."

"I'm really sorry," I whisper, wishing Raj had never even dropped the box off, or that Mom had never wanted the book in the first place.

"It's not your fault," Sae says with an understanding smile, maybe the most chill immortal ever. "How were you to know?"

I take the now-badly-crumpled scroll from my pocket. There are small pieces of wax still attached to it. I hand it over, feeling sheepish. "We were trying to figure out how to make it bring us home again."

"The scroll itself doesn't have the power to bring you home." Sae reads it quickly, then tucks it into their straw basket, deep among magical plants and flowers so it won't fall out. Something smooth and pale green gleams from inside the basket—the immortal's famous jade clappers. "Though the emperor had to use it for you to cross over."

"I guess that's what caused the earthquake," Marilla says, padding over now that Howl's asleep on the grass. "And the clock on my phone to stop working."

"That was me," Erlang says. "As the god of engineering, I'm able to keep time still. Since mortals often make decisions based on time, we didn't want you distracted by anything that might be happening in your realm. Once you beat Chaos and return home, your time will continue again as though it never stopped."

I grab my phone from my pocket and check. Just like Marilla's, the clock on the screen is stuck at the same time, which is right after Erlang's earthquake. I send a test text to my group chat with Libby and Jasper, but it stays unsent, which means we're offline here, too. Not even the camera or flashlight works. Home should only be minutes away, but it might as well be on another planet.

"I guess our technology just isn't Zhen compatible," Marilla says.

I'm trying not to feel trapped even as familiar fingers of anxiety come to life behind my ribs. I slip my phone into my backpack—no use for it now. "How long do I have to fix everything?"

"Not long," Sae admits. "As Chaos grows stronger, we'll also grow weaker."

"But it's my choice, right?" Otherwise, why would they worry about us having reasons to leave, like Mom and Dad wondering where we are by now?

"It is. Even if you are the one who broke the seal, we can't make you stay. Your heart must be complete in wanting to stop Chaos if you are to defeat him. You must believe in yourself and the task."

"You have to say yes," Marilla hisses as she circles my feet. "You're the only one who can save Zhen!"

I look at her. How can I believe I can do this? Because between the two of us, I'm not the brave sister. Here's where the Xu Glue stops working.

Sae's dark eyes lock on mine. "So, will you help us, Astrid Xu?"

SIX

A cold, prickly feeling makes my shoulders twitch. Marilla, Sae, Erlang, Howl—the weight of all their stares feels like the audience all over again, watching me mess up. Knowing this is my fault tastes like panic stuck in my throat. Even thinking about fighting a demon makes my lungs want to shrivel up.

I don't think I can do this. The Scroll of Chaos might be true, but it's also a lie if it's decided I'm the only one who can stop the prophecy. It needs someone better, more capable. Stronger.

Then Sae says softly: "If you help us, we'll help you save your mother."

I stare at them in surprise. "How do you know she's sick?"

"You've been asking Zao Jun for help," Erlang says. "The Kitchen God. He informed the Jade Emperor."

"The Kitchen God's been listening? And just ignored me?" My stomach sinks. Marilla was right—I've been wasting my time.

"Jun hears all, but only reports some. As deities, we try not to interfere in matters beyond our own realm or get involved in mortal matters."

"Why? You all have powers. You can help so much."

"Because if things go wrong, mortals would blame us. And if things go right, mortals would say they never needed us at all. When the truth is likely somewhere in between."

"But now you're offering to help mortals because you need *me* to help *you*."

"Of course." Erlang shrugs. "We are trying to make you an offer that you can't refuse."

"My mother for your realm."

"What you hold dearly for what we hold dearly."

"How would you help my mom?" An offer from an immortal and a demigod warrior isn't something that's going to happen every day. Sure, I would still have to save a realm, but—

"The prophecy says you must get to the top of Kunlun Mountain," Sae says. "That's where we'll find the weapon— the 'chance,' as mentioned in the scroll. You'll need it to fight Chaos. Also on the mountain is the Queen Mother of the West's sacred garden, with all its plants of magic. If you defeat Chaos, she'll grant you, a mortal, a rare audience. You can then make your plea for something from her garden."

My breath catches.

Because what's magic but another kind of medicine?

And not just regular medicine but medicine from the gods? The fog that won't leave Mom—there's no way it can beat *magic* . . . right?

But which plant would I ask for? What kind of medicine that wouldn't just get rid of Mom's depression but make her better in every other way, too?

The answer blooms in my mind, as bright as the paintings that hang on our walls at home. And I know exactly how I'm going to save Mom.

"An immortal peach," I say to Sae. "That's what I'll ask for."

"A peach?" Marilla sounds doubtful. "I don't know . . ."

"Yes! It'll be like how Mom always makes us eat peaches on our birthdays."

"So we can live long and happy lives. I know the drill. But do you really think it can make Mom better forever?"

"That's the plan," I say. "Besides, even if it doesn't make her better forever, it'll still help. We can't ever be immortal, but the next best thing is to not die for a long, long, time, right?"

A look passes between us, and I know what my sister is thinking because I'm thinking the same thing (and it's something neither of us has ever said out loud). It's how we both know that for some people stuck deep in fog, they can become so desperate to escape, they start to believe there's only one way out.

Marilla headbutts my leg, then grins at me. It reminds me of how she used to grin at me when she was younger, before she began to leave me alone, too. "I can't wait for Xiwangmu to give it to you! Maybe there'll even be a ceremony!"

"I wish I could guarantee that she will," Sae says. "But the Queen Mother agrees only to hear your request. She will be grateful, of course, but we can't speak for her."

"Well, she's given immortal peaches to mortals before, right?" Marilla asks.

"A few," Erlang says. "However, those were emperors, and it was thousands of years ago. She hasn't been moved to gift any since. Not to discourage you, but it would be wrong of us to soften the facts."

So, no guarantees.

And I might not even come close to beating Chaos.

But . . . I also might. I *have* to believe I can. And I'll have Sae and Erlang and Howl to help me. Plus, when else will I ever get so close to magic that's also medicine? It's like all signs are pointing to yes and I'd be foolish to pass this up.

To save Mom, I have to save the realm. That's it.

I take a deep breath, wishing my lungs didn't still feel

tight. It's doubt, crowding out my air. My old fear of messing up again. But I also feel different this time, and it's because I'm excited, too. I feel a thick and wild hope that's like staring at too-bright stars—hard to look at, nearly impossible to stop.

I turn to Sae and Erlang. "It's a deal."

Sae flashes a smile that reminds me that they're not that much older than Marilla and me. As much a kid as a powerful immortal. "I promise we'll get you home safely."

Erlang pats the bow and arrow at his waist. "Don't worry, mortal. You'll have plenty of help to make up for your natural weaknesses and lack of fighting ability."

"Um, thanks for the vote of confidence?"

"You're welcome," he replies, not picking up on my sarcasm at all. I'll just have to prove him wrong, somehow.

Sae lays their hoe over their shoulder, straw basket bobbing from the end. "We'll keep westward the entire journey, toward Kunlun Mountain."

Howl barks and stands in front of Marilla. Starlight gleams off the gold armor on the dog's back as he waits. His expression is just like Bear's whenever the dog grabs his leash and drags it over to Jasper, as if to say, "Let's go, human."

"I think he's offering you a ride," I say to Marilla, laughing. "The grass *is* taller than you."

She gives me a quick scowl, but a second later she's perched on top of Howl's back, smug as only cats can be. "My very own Uber dog," she says.

"Seems you've gained another companion animal, Erlang," Sae says.

Erlang gives his dog a disgruntled look. "Thousands of creatures to befriend and you pick a mortal cat?"

"Follow me," Sae says, ignoring Erlang, and walks into the cluster of trees.

"Hold on, we're not going to wait until morning?" I call out after them. Isn't that what everyone does when it's dark out?

"We can go by starlight for a bit longer," they call back from inside the woods.

"Your mortal need for sleep will slow us down," Erlang adds. "We have to make up for it while we can." A sharp grin. "Besides, grassy fields such as this aren't good for sleeping, anyway. Not when rats and snakes are partial to them." With a swish of his red cape, Erlang also disappears into the trees.

Howl—with Marilla still on his back—follows right behind him. Their matching gold armor flashes and winks.

"C'mon, Astrid!" Marilla yells back to me from the shadows. "You can't change your mind now!"

"I'm not!" I won't. I *can't.*

I go after them, imagining rats and snakes at my ankles, aiming to bite.

• • •

"Do you think we'll get statues in Zhen if we stop the prophecy?" Marilla asks sometime later as she rides along. "Maybe the Jade Emperor will even put them outside his palace."

Erlang snorts. "Considering I only have a couple of statues myself despite fighting in hundreds of battles over thousands of years for the realm, don't get your hopes up."

"But you'll ask, right?"

"We'll be sure to propose the idea," Sae promises.

The trees keep growing thicker as we walk, as though we're zeroing in on some heart of the forest. Keeping behind everyone else, I reach out and touch swaying branches as I pass. Trunks loom close and I trace their bark with my fingers. The ground goes from grass to leaves and dirt; if I listen carefully, I can hear tiny creatures scampering across. Friends of Erlang's rats and snakes, I think.

This part of Zhen seems a lot like home. If I blur out the too-bright stars, it's almost like camping at one of the local lakes. Marilla and I would be in our tent and staring up at the skylight, imagining the wild animals roaming the area (where no sound was ever truly scary). We haven't gone camping in years, but now we'd probably just argue the entire time.

Still, every step forward means one step closer to Kunlun Mountain. Most of me can't wait. I know that once I see it, it'll be like Mom's paintings coming to life, the stories I grew up with turning into reality. I'll go back home and tell her everything, make her keep wanting to hear new stories. And for the small part of me that can wait? I'll make sure it stays small. I won't let it grow and change all my excitement into fear.

I'm mid-yawn when something catches on the top of my backpack. I stop walking and reach up for the branch to push it away.

It's a skinny twig. Half of it's a mottled white. Like snow without its luster, or dull bones. I remember Grandma telling us how in Chinese culture, white means death. It feels cold against my fingers.

Watching the field fall under Chaos's spell was like watching it happen through a window. But now that I'm actually touching grim magic, it feels so much more powerful. Like I'm holding a cage with a trapped animal. I shiver and let go of the branch, rubbing my hand off on my jeans. All of Zhen like this? It's hard to imagine.

"We're crossing paths with Chaos."

I glance up. It's Sae, coming back with the others. The immortal reaches for the branch and snaps it off. "The demon flew over here on his way down from Kunlun," they say, pointing toward the sky.

I look up—Sae's right. The top of the tree's lost all its color and turned as pale as the moon.

"He won't be coming back this way, then, right?" Still on Howl's back, Marilla's whiskers tremble. "Since he's already cast his spell here?"

"Hopefully not." Sae examines the branch, their expression unsettled. "He's spreading his magic as fast as he can over the realm—he'll likely not go over old ground if he can help it."

Erlang takes the branch and shows Marilla and me the center. It's a bright green inside.

I'm surprised. "It's still alive!"

"Yes, it's only asleep. It's what happens when Chaos absorbs someone or something's qi—their life force, their life energy. By stealing qi from everything around him, the demon continues to grow stronger."

"Qi also means the natural balance of things," I say. Grandma used to tell us about this, too: "When everything is working right, that is qi," she said. "Winter is cold, but that is why spring is warm. Death comes, but life always gets to happen first."

Erlang passes me the branch.

I take it carefully. Now that I know it's still alive, it doesn't feel so cold anymore. Its bright green center feels defiant, holding on despite everything. Spring over winter. Life before death. Sun instead of fog. *Qi finding a way, Mom.*

We start moving through the trees again.

Sae nods. "Qi *is* also about balance. Not just the balance of someone's life force, but of the entire universe. All of it must stay in balance for its source to stay healthy. It's why we need to stop Chaos as soon as possible. The realm is very quickly growing weak."

"What about *our* qi?" Marilla asks. "Astrid's and mine. Is he going to steal ours, too?" Her ears flick over and over, the universal cat sign for wondering.

"Being other-realm means you're safe for now. But the universe is a giant wheel made up of wheels of worlds, and the wheel of this world links all its realms together. So even as our qi is different, it's also connected. It won't be long before Chaos senses your qi and tries to steal it, too."

"But he'll be stealing from us first," Erlang says. "And once I grow too weak, my hold on your realm's time will start to slip forward. The sooner we beat Chaos, the better for everyone."

I picture everything back home running again and

Mom and Dad discovering that Marilla and I are missing. What if they call the police? How would we explain how we were off in a mythological world to stop a gigantic flood?

"If Chaos made his way down from the top of Kunlun Mountain, then everyone there must already be under his spell, right?" I ask. "Including the Jade Emperor."

"Yes, along with the rest of the realm's gods and goddesses," Sae says. "Everyone was gathered at the royal palace, which is the emperor's home when he's away from the Heavens. It was a party to celebrate the spring harvest, and Jun had just arrived with his latest report for the emperor. He was actually in the middle of telling us about *you*, Astrid, and your latest request for help, when the demon was reborn. When we realized you were also the one who broke the seal, the emperor used his power to bring you—and Marilla, it turns out—to Zhèn. Then, before grim magic could fully overcome him, he assigned Erlang and me to find you both and guide you to Kunlun. We managed to leave just in time, but the rest of the palace wasn't so lucky. All our family and friends are now under Chaos's spell."

"He had no physical form yet, then," Erlang says. "Not even the shadow cloud you two saw earlier. But that will change as he continues to steal qi from the realm. Kunlun is now where his power is strongest, and chaos will spread from there to the rest of Zhen, like a great spider descending from its web and hunting in all directions."

"Gross," Marilla says, her tail whipping back and forth in the air. "Maybe that's what Chaos is growing into: a giant spider."

"It might be," Sae admits. "We know the prophecy, but the demon itself is new to us. We'll find out soon enough." They glance around the woods as we walk. "By then, everything here will be without color, the realm a shell of itself. And then the flood will come."

I carefully tuck the branch into a still-living shrub. "Then let's walk faster."

SEVEN

"We've covered enough ground for tonight." Erlang steps into a natural clearing between the trees. "How about here?"

Sae looks around and nods. "It's open but not *too* open."

"Cool, we'll see Chaos coming before he sees us." Marilla does her Bruce Lee kick, cat legs splaying. "Not that I'm scared."

"Oh, there are other creatures in this part of the realm." Erlang grins, and his teeth gleam in the night just like his armor does. "More than just rats and snakes. Grim magic won't have put them all to sleep yet."

Marilla eyes him like she's considering another one of her kicks. "You'll finally get to fight something instead of just talking about it."

"Maybe you'll pick up some tricks, *mortal*."

"*You're* the famous warrior, not me."

Everyone claims a tree inside the small clearing. Mine's got low-lying branches—perfect as an overhead canopy. And there are patches of soft moss all around— not too shabby. I drop my backpack to the ground, unable to stop another huge yawn. Everyone else collapses just as tiredly. Sae and Erlang might even sleep, although they don't actually need to.

The stars are mini stoplights shining down through the trees. I search for and find the moon, the same one I'd be seeing through my bedroom window. Homesickness and worry tickle the backs of my eyes and I wonder how Mom's doing. If Erlang freezing time means she's getting a break from the fog or if it's just left her stuck in it.

"How will we get home afterward?" I ask. "The Jade Emperor just creates another door?"

"He could," Sae says, "but he won't have to." They take something from their basket and hold them out. Three large gems. They look like the world's biggest emeralds, sparkling beneath the starlight.

"Wow, those are *pretty*." Marilla leaps across the clearing to see and I jump up after her.

"Dragon scales," Sae tells us as we ooh and aah. They sit in the middle of their palm, dark green and shiny. "Their navigational power makes it easier to travel between realms. We would have used them to bring you here, but Chaos was already at the palace, so the emperor had to act quickly. Only he has the power to build such a bridge; any other deity would have failed."

"So how come I ended up a cat?" Marilla asks.

"Our guess is that his magic might have only accounted

for one mortal being, not two, and adjusted last minute. The emperor would be able to tell you for sure, but he's asleep."

My sister moans. "Think of all the many amazing creatures I could have been instead. Like a qilin, or a trickster fox!"

"She'll change back when we go home, right?" I ask.

"As long as you travel back with a dragon scale," Sae replies.

"Not traveling with one is also why you arrived where you did," Erlang says from beneath his tree. Howl is sprawled out beside him, head on his paws. "A dragon scale allows for accuracy. It's good we found you two when we did."

"Like when Dad gets lost because bad Wi-Fi keeps messing up the directions on his phone," Marilla says. "You can end up anywhere."

"What's Wi-Fi?" Sae asks.

I think of how to explain. "It's kind of like having a map. But imagine losing it and deciding to keep going anyway."

"Ah. Then I agree—doing that here, you can also end up on the other side of Zhen." Sae tips the dragon scales into my hand.

Their smoothness feels like glass against my skin.

They're also warm, as though there's fire inside. Marilla touches her paw to one and oohs and aahs some more.

"Does everybody in Zhen get one?" I ask, passing them back to Sae, who returns them to their basket. I picture Zhen's gods and goddesses zipping around from one realm to another, the same way we travel using planes or trains or ships (one definitely seems cooler).

"No," Erlang says. "Dragon scales are very rare and very valuable. Only my uncle is allowed to gift them or lend them out."

When I yawn again—which makes Marilla yawn—Erlang declares, "Sleep. You need to refuel your weakened mortal bodies."

My sister rolls her eyes, but we don't argue as we head back toward our trees.

"Good night," Sae says, tucking their hands into the silk sleeves of their robe. Beside them is their hoe and basket. "If anyone does see a rat or snake, it's because Erlang summoned them."

"And we leave at dawn." The warrior sets his helmet on the ground. His black hair is slicked back, and on his forehead is his truth-seeing eye that I saw a hint of earlier. It's shut, but it's definitely the same eye that's on his painting at home.

Marilla crosses the clearing again to see. And because I can't pass up this chance to get a closer look at the famous third eye, I get up, too.

"Does it only open when you want it to see a truth?" Marilla whispers, not wanting to bug Sae.

"Yes." Erlang lays down his sword and bow, and Howl curls up next to them. "It wears on me to have it see more than it needs to."

"Can you ask it just *one* truth?"

The eye blinks open, a bigger version of one of Erlang's regular eyes. It peers first at Marilla and then me. "Fine. One."

For a second, I think she might ask about Mom, and I can't decide if I'm relieved or not when she says: "Will the prophecy come true?"

Erlang shakes his head. "My eye seeks truth from lies, penetrates far distances and through mist. But it doesn't see the future." He draws his red cape over himself, all the way up over his head. "Dawn," his voice emerges. Five seconds later, he and Howl are snoring in unison.

Marilla comes over to my tree instead of going over to hers.

"Well, maybe it's better not to know," she says as I unzip my backpack and take out my inhaler.

"How could you not want to know? How would

you know what to do, then?" I take my usual two-puffs-at-bedtime and rinse out my mouth (even if it's just with spit).

An awkward cat-style shrug. "Because it'd be really, really hard knowing you can't do anything at all?"

"There's always something you can do."

Marilla's ears flick hard. "No, that's just untrue. There isn't, not always."

I busy myself putting away my inhaler so I don't have to talk anymore. My sister might be a cat, but she's also still definitely Marilla; we're not talking about Mom, but we might as well be. Irritated, I grab her track pants from my backpack, lie down beneath my canopy of branches, and drag the pants on top of me like a blanket.

"You're going to get them dirty!" Marilla tries to paw them off me.

"They're already dirty from being all over the grass."

"Not dirty enough that they need to get even *more* dirty! Put them back!"

"Ugh, fine." I push them into my bag and lie back down. I shut my eyes. "Good night."

She hisses sharply and moves away.

• • •

I'm already asleep when something pokes me in the side.

"Astrid, I can't sleep!" Marilla whispers.

Remembering I'm supposed to be annoyed, I mutter, "Try harder."

"I miss home. Do you think Mom and Dad are okay?"

I open my eyes. Marilla's leaning right over me, the triangles of her ears haloed by starlight.

"Yeah, I do," I say, not wanting her to know I'm worried, too. "They don't even know we're gone." Feeling bad now about being annoyed, I whisper, "Want to sleep over here?"

She steps onto my stomach (probably on purpose; I don't blame her) before plopping down next to my shoulder. "Who's Fuxi? The scroll talks about him, but I can't remember the myth, and I should probably know it if it becomes important later, right?"

"I thought you didn't like mythology anymore."

"I don't like it as *much*."

Maybe she's right—the scroll must mention Fuxi for a reason.

"I can't tell the story as well as Mom can," I say, sitting up and reaching for my backpack. "But we can read it together if you want." It'll be nearly like old times, mythology instead of arguing.

In a minute, we're both on our stomachs, *A Handbook of Ancient Chinese Myths* opened up on the ground in front of us. We have to read by starlight since the flashlights on our phones don't work, but it's okay since the stars are so bright.

Fuxi the Creator

Over two thousand years ago, the mortal Lady Huaxu stepped in a giant footprint pressed into the earth. Soon she discovered that she would have a child, and because the footprint had been left behind by the God of Thunder, her child was born a demigod. She named him Fuxi.

As he grew older, Fuxi began to compare life in the Heavens to life in the mortal realm. He saw how gods and goddesses lived with order while humans were scattered and without direction. Fuxi decided he would do his best to help humans live fuller lives.

The demigod became an inventor and passed down his knowledge to humans. He created marriage and laws. He invented coins out of copper and cloth that he called silk. He crafted weapons and nets and taught people how to hunt and fish. He imagined up cooking so humans could enjoy hot food. He showed them writing so they could record their stories and then share them.

Fuxi was mostly happy about his work. But he felt something was missing and decided to find it.

He walked through the mortal realm, looking for clues. Soon, a pair of phoenixes flew across the sky. He noticed that they would rest only on the branches of a great parasol tree, even though there were many buildings nearby. When the phoenixes began to sing their songs over the tree, Fuxi realized he wanted to invent music for mortals.

To create the worthiest of instruments, he knew the wood would have to come from the parasol tree. Fuxi cut a branch from its middle—too high and the wood would not echo; too low and the wood would not ring. From this wood he crafted a stringed musical instrument. Hearing the notes filled him with a sense of balance and harmony. Fuxi then taught mortals how to craft their own instrument from more parasol trees and how to play. And that is why today, music still fills humans with great joy.

Marilla yawns so all her cat teeth show. "I think I remember bits of that story now. But it was still nice to read the whole thing again."

"It's Mom's book; I bet she'll let you read it whenever you want," I say casually as I close it. "Just be careful with it because it's really old."

"Sure, maybe. Hmm, I wonder how reaching the parasol trees at the top of Kunlun Mountain will help you beat Chaos. The scroll said that."

"It did, but I'm not sure. Maybe Sae or Erlang will know." It's too late to think about a demon anymore, and

I get comfortable on the moss again. "We'd better go to sleep now. Erlang will bug us all day tomorrow if we complain about being tired."

Marilla huddles closer to my shoulder. "Do you think I should go back?" Her voice somehow sounds small, like she's younger. "What if I get in the way or do something so that you can't stop the prophecy? I'm only here by accident. And I *was* trying to take the scroll from you when you broke the seal. It's not even all your fault."

"I'm still the one who broke it in the end. And I was holding your hand when we came through. You couldn't help it."

"The emperor still only meant to bring you."

A part of me thinks she *should* go back. I'm the one who broke the seal, not her. She could be safe at home with Mom and Dad. And I know it's Sae and Erlang and Howl who will be able to help the most just because they have magic and we don't. I wouldn't be alone.

Except I think I'd *feel* alone. I never told Marilla, but those times when she couldn't fall sleep because of Mom until she slept with me? It was always easier for me to fall asleep, too.

"You can't leave," I say. "I'll be too scared if you go. I know I'm going to need your help."

"How could I help? I'm a *cat.*"

"Cats are useful."

"*How?*"

"Um . . . you can run faster than any of us, and not just because you're a track star when you're human, but because cats are also super fast. And you don't have asthma like me so you have nothing to slow you down. You're also tiny, so if we need to fit somewhere—"

She swats at me. "These are all silly reasons!" But I can tell she's not really upset. "Okay, I'll stay. I *want* to help, even if I can't be the one who has to fight Chaos. I know I'll find a way to help you."

"I think so, too."

"Are you mortals done being loud?" Erlang sounds grumpy from inside his cape, which is still draped over his head. "For the love of the emperor, go to sleep!"

I quickly slide the handbook into my backpack, both Marilla and I trying not to laugh.

She's asleep in minutes, and I fall asleep right after.

My dreams are bad.

I climb a mountain, and right before I reach the top, another mountain grows and I have to start over again.

I climb a mountain, completely out of breath, already late to meet the demon. And when I grab my rescue inhaler, it turns as white as bone.

I climb a mountain, and there is the demon at its top,

and its face is made up of hundreds of pairs of eyes, waiting for me to fail.

I enter a garden, the Queen Mother of the West is inside, and this is what she says to me as she smiles: "You might have saved Zhen, Astrid Xu. But I will never gift an immortal peach to you, for who is it that put the realm in danger in the first place?"

EIGHT

"Astrid, wake up!" Little cat paws knead my head. "It's already dawn!" More kneading. "Are you awake?"

"Nope." I push away the tail that's swishing in my face. I'm not a morning person, but Marilla's used to getting up early for track practice.

"I'm going to go wake up the others," she says, racing away.

I crack my eyes open.

A dark purple sky overhead. Still-bright stars. The kind of cool feeling in the air that only happens in the earliest parts of the morning. Across the clearing, Marilla chases Howl into the woods. Sae and Erlang are still sleeping.

I shut my eyes again, wondering if I can sneak five more minutes of sleep, when the worst of the bad dreams rushes back.

Xiwangmu, the Queen Mother of the West, declaring she will never give me an immortal peach.

The memory is like a jolt of bad energy; I'm now wide-awake but feel sick at the same time. What if the dream actually comes true? Sae *did* say there were no guarantees, but I guess I never really believed that. I thought there couldn't be anything bigger than saving the realm, so of course Xiwangmu would reward me with whatever I asked for. I never really thought about the other half of it—that bringing Chaos to life in the first place was just as big.

I shut my eyes harder, trying to wipe away the dream even as it plays out again in my head. Thoughts are racing. *Mom, I'll come up with something, I promise!*

If I can't stop the Queen Mother from saying no, then I'll just have to fix the problem before that happens.

I have to steal an immortal peach.

I pull myself up, cold all over as my heart pounds. I fumble for my inhaler and take my regular morning puffs (two, just like at bedtime), telling myself I can't be serious.

The rule in Chinese mythology is that no one can steal the gift of immortality without being punished—and mythological punishments are famous for being over the top. Chang'e is the beautiful wife of Hou Yi the archer. After he saves the entire world from going up in flames, Xiwangmu rewards him with the elixir of immortality. But Chang'e takes it herself and is exiled to the moon for eternity. Then there's the trickster Monkey King, who feasts on stolen peaches and ends up being buried in a fiery cauldron for forty-nine days. After he escapes, he's banished beneath a mountain for five hundred years.

But . . . the Queen Mother would never have to know, I realize. Her magical garden is on the way to the top of Kunlun Mountain; by the time I wake her up by beating Chaos, I'll already have stolen the peach. I'll bring it home and Mom will be saved.

Feeling better (but also guilty), I tuck my inhaler back into my bag.

"No!"

I look up, startled.

Sae's yelling in their sleep. "The water!" they shout next. Then they sit up straight, their eyes wide and their face pale. "It's— I can't—"

The immortal's scared of water?

Erlang tosses his cape off his head, instantly awake. "Sae, wake up, it's just a dream. You're safe."

Sae rubs their eyes, then blinks. They take a deep breath. "Thank you."

I pick up my backpack and cross the small clearing. I want to tell them that talking about bad dreams can make them less scary, but I can't, since I don't want to talk about mine. "Nightmares are the worst."

Sae gets up and brushes off their silk robe. They smile at me, though they still seem a bit shaken. "They are. Good morning, Astrid."

"Good morning. I didn't know immortals dreamed."

"We can. Other than the ability-to-never-die part, we're probably more like mortals than you think."

Erlang slips his sword over his back. "Let's not go *that* far."

Sae passes out sprigs from their basket that we chew to clean our teeth. Now that it's closer to day than night, I see more of the realm that's in Mom's paintings. Trees topped with leaves that look like green lace. The ground that's a patchwork of dark brown soil and sea-blue moss. Only the dull white parts don't belong.

As Marilla and Howl chase each other through the trees (who knew she'd become BFFs with a mythological dog?), Sae and Erlang study the scroll.

"What do these mean?" I point to the drawings along the top: the bird's wing, bird's head, and feather. "Can they be clues for something?"

"The drawings together represent the phoenix," Sae explains. "Phoenixes fly over the parasol trees in the myth of Fuxi, and it's the parasol trees at the top of Kunlun Mountain that we need to get to. But all that is already mentioned in the prophecy itself."

"Artwork, then, and likely nothing more." Erlang puts on his helmet and whistles. Howl races over, Marilla still chasing.

Sae rolls up the scroll and tucks it back into their straw basket. "It's nearly morning; time to go."

I peer upward. The dark purple of the sky is changing to a pale pink. A second later, there's blue mixing in, and a hazy gold coin pops up along the horizon. The sun. I glance over at Marilla. She's watching as carefully as I am, and I wonder if she's remembering Mom telling her the myth of Fusang.

The sun climbs and climbs.

I notice how hot the air's becoming. Like there's a giant stove nearby and someone's cranking it up. I wipe a film of sweat from my forehead and try not to worry—because it's not just things like dust and pollen and animal fur that can make asthma act up, but also weather. For me, hot air is never great.

A dry snapping sound crackles across the air. A second later, there's another: SNAP.

Erlang frowns and glances around. "What's that?"

We all look, and I spot it first. It's the ground—it's cracking apart. Long, thin lines crisscross it, like lightning's striking the earth and all the zigzags of it are getting stuck in there. It's also drying up—as I watch, the rich brown soil goes gray; sea-blue moss shrivels up into crispy fluff. The trees surrounding the clearing start to smoke, as though set on fire by that imaginary stove.

Right away, I think it's Chaos. Except that nothing is turning white. And the way the moss is drying up is just like Dad's attempts at gardening. He always forgets to water stuff, so all his plants end up just as dead looking.

"It's the air," I blurt out. "It's getting too hot, too fast, and drying everything up!"

Sae looks troubled. "This area isn't known for droughts."

"And no drought moves at this speed," Erlang adds.

"The sun's changing color!" Marilla calls out.

Thirst from the heat stings my throat as the coin of gold turns pumpkin orange, bright as fire. A sizzling sound fills the air.

Bam!

The sun bursts apart and becomes a great bird of fire, its long feathers vivid oranges and reds. The bird flies across the sky, feathers behind it like dancing flames. A second later, more suns are climbing upward and bursting into fiery birds. They all zip around, fireballs burning trails into the blue sky. One bird drops low and dives over trees, setting them on fire. Another bird swoops along the ground; more cracks split open.

I quickly count them: ten suns, burning up the earth.

Marilla and I look at each other. "Astrid, this is—"

"Hou Yi's myth!" I yell.

One of the birds flies right over us, and Marilla squeals.

"Into my cape!" Erlang tells her.

My sister doesn't need to be told twice. She leaps onto his red cape, and using her cat claws, she scampers up and hides in its folds. "Hou Yi's golden ravens." Sae watches the flaming birds zoom around the sky. Smoke and ash trail in all directions. "But I suspect these are Chaos's version. Firebirds."

"He's creating chaos," Erlang growls. At his side, Howl barks up a storm, furious that he can't reach any of the firebirds. The dog's golden armor goes orange as it reflects the fire-filled sky. "He's rewriting Zhen's stories because he wants new endings, ones that will unbalance the realm's life. Fighting them will use up our energy. It's all part of his plan!"

"But we can't just ignore it," I say, coughing. Already my skin feels sunburned. "If this is supposed to be Hou Yi's myth, the realm will burn up. We have to shoot down the suns!"

Erlang notches his bow and arrow and aims for one of the firebirds. A second later a black arrow climbs toward the sky. But before it can reach the bird, the arrow disintegrates and turns into a puff of smoke.

"The targets are too hot." Erlang swears and sets his bow and arrow back at his waist. "Even for my arrows that can withstand dragon fire."

Marilla pops her head out of his cape. "What about your third eye? It can shoot lasers right through mountains!"

He throws an exasperated look over his shoulder. "Mortal, you cannot believe every far-fetched story you hear. Lasers? Ridiculous!"

"What about transforming?" Sae turns to him. "Can you change into one of Hou Yi's arrows? I can use your bow."

"Let me try." The warrior shuts his eyes, focusing. But instead of turning into a golden arrow, his eyes flash open.

"I can't transform," Erlang snarls. His face flushes red. "Just like I can't see quite as far anymore, or as sharply or truthfully. Chaos is stealing my qi."

My stomach twists. Soon he and Sae and Howl will be as powerless as the rest of Zhen's sleeping immortals and magical creatures. How much longer before Chaos is the strongest of all?

Alarm darkens Sae's face. "Maybe nothing but Hou Yi's arrows will work, arrows we have no time to re-create."

Not to mention that magical tigers and enchanted snakes only live on Kunlun Mountain, I think. Which we definitely haven't reached yet. *If only we could make our own version of Hou Yi's arrows . . .*

"Wait!" I say, thinking fast. "If Chaos is just writing new versions of Zhen's myths, then the firebirds are all him. What if we don't need the original weapon to destroy them?"

"It's certainly worth a try." Sae crouches down and starts searching through their basket. All different kinds of flowers and herbs spill out, scenting the heated air. The immortal grins at me. "As powerful as Erlang's arrows are, they still aren't magic. And if Chaos used magic to create the firebirds, then—"

"It'll have to be magic to help destroy them!" I grin back.

"Exactly. Astrid, you'll have to help us."

My grin disappears. Help? There's a whole lot more at stake here than a school concert if I mess up. "But I don't have any powers."

Ash swirls down from the sky. There's more smoke in the air now, too (which isn't going to do my asthma any favors, either).

"Are you really powerless as long as you keep trying?" Sae asks. "The search for strength ends only when you stop looking."

"It's time to see what you can do." Erlang gives me a look that says despite being a warrior, he somehow understands my fear: *Are you as weak as we feared, or stronger?*

Sae gets back to their feet, something clutched in their hand. They glance at my backpack. "What do you have inside there?"

"Um, a book, my medicine, and my clarinet."

"A clarinet?"

"A musical instrument. It's what I play in school band."

Sae's eyes light up. "Can you show it to me?"

"Okay, sure?" Sae's sense of timing seems kind of weird, given the firebirds zooming around over our heads. But Zhen *is* their world—they must know what they're doing. I slip off my backpack, take out my clarinet case, and quickly put my clarinet together. I play an easy note for them.

My E rings out, deep and true.

Sae nods. "Perfect. You're going to need it in a second."

"What?" Tight breathlessness blooms in my chest. To actually play in front of *the* Lan Caihe and Erlang Shen when I can't even make myself play with a bunch of other kids? Overhead, the firebirds continue to swoop and dive. More of the ground cracks apart. Trees in the distance crackle and snap.

"It's how you're going to help us fight the firebirds. Being skilled at something is a form of power."

I shake my head. Me being powerful at clarinet? No way. "Listen, I only play because of my asthma. To help with my breathing."

Sae smiles. "Power comes in all forms." They hold out what they've been clutching.

On their palm are three tufts of grass. I don't know much about plants (other than Dad needs to start remembering to water), but I'm pretty sure I've never seen red-and-black-striped grass before.

Erlang peers closely. "Yao grass?"

"A type of it, yes," Sae says. "This type has transmuting powers."

"Ooh, maybe your book talks about yao grass, Astrid!" Marilla calls out. She's back on the ground and poking at my backpack. I reach over and take out the handbook for her. She paws through the pages, then stops. "Here it is! Listen." She begins to read:

Yao Grass

Yao grass is a plant with magical properties. One of the more common varieties helps create feelings of romantic love, and upon eating the plant, a person will find themselves easily attracting the love of others. A second common type helps keep the mind clear of confusion and tangled thoughts. A third, much rarer type is known for its transmuting capabilities, temporarily changing one's most powerful asset into another form.

I hold up my clarinet. "*This* is going to somehow become a weapon?"

"Trust the yao grass," Sae says. "It senses your strengths and knows exactly what to do. Now, eat it fast, before these suns start burning us up, too."

NINE

I stuff a tuft of yao grass in my mouth, chew (it's vaguely minty), and swallow. Sae and Erlang eat theirs, too.

Sae's basket changes first. It's now a straw-colored bow, its accompanying arrows the colors of the basket's flowers and herbs. And instead of leveling up his existing bow and arrow set, Erlang's got a *second* one, bright and gleaming gold. It's his triple-pointed spear—the yao grass knew to transmute Erlang's most powerful strength.

I glance down at my clarinet, expecting my own personalized bow and arrow. But it hasn't changed at all. Still the same old clarinet. I stare at it like it's betrayed me somehow.

"It seems your power is strongest through playing your clarinet, Astrid," Sae says. "The yao grass would know otherwise."

Before I can ask how playing music is going to help bring down the firebirds, Erlang nocks one of his golden arrows. He aims and lets the golden arrow go. It flies through the air as quick as lightning. I catch only a glimpse of it before it's gone from sight. In the next second, a firebird screeches, goes dark, and fades away as a trail of smoke.

Marilla—who's now perched on Erlang's shoulder—whoops like she's front row at a show. Howl's excited, too, bounding all around the warrior's feet.

"One down," Erlang says, clearly pleased with himself.

Sae pulls back on their bow. A pale blue arrow arcs high from it, zooming in on a firebird.

Poof. The creature burns out. Nothing but smoke.

"Two!" Erlang yells cheerfully. "Chaos won't like this one bit."

"He'll know now that someone is trying to stop him," Sae says. "He'll be on the lookout."

My throat goes tight at the memory of Chaos over the trees, the menacing doom of his windstorm. Can playing clarinet really match up to that kind of power? The instrument feels odd in my hand, as though I've never held it before.

Erlang shoots another arrow. This one misses, the firebird too fast.

"Astrid, play!" Marilla shouts. "You're not going to mess up, okay?"

Trust the yao grass.

Power comes in all forms.

Before I can start thinking about audiences, I take a deep breath, so deep it comes from beneath that tight, pinched feeling still in my chest, and start playing "Path of the Wind."

The first thing I notice is how quiet I sound in the open air—I've never played outdoors before. I blow a tiny bit harder so my playing gets louder, careful to pay attention to my breathing. I feel kind of silly, just standing and playing music while Sae and Erlang get to shoot actual arrows. What if yao grass just made its first mistake of a transmutation in the history of mythological transmutation? But I keep playing, skipping over the high notes like I've been doing in class for months, certain that no one in Zhen will mind too much.

Something drifts out of the end of my clarinet.

It's shiny and silver and about the size of a dime. Not solid, though. Instead, it's just an image, formed out of the air that traveled from my lungs and along my clarinet. It's perfectly weightless, too—I can tell by the way it floats up into the sky. It glimmers and flashes as it goes, as reflective as a mirror.

As the silvery image floats past one of the zooming firebirds, the creature goes dead still mid-flight. It doesn't move and seems almost frozen by the shininess. When the silvery image shrinks up and disappears a second later, the firebird shakes itself and starts swooping across the sky again.

"Astrid!" Sae calls out, grinning at me. "Now you know what to do!"

And I have to grin back because I do. I knew as soon as I saw that firebird freeze.

I start playing again, excitement helping my lungs fill. So that they feel fuller than they have in a long time. Not close to perfect, but still better.

Another silvery image tugs free from my clarinet. This time it forms into a bigger and brighter mirror, and it floats up and up. It winks as it goes, like a spinning disco ball at a party. It flashes orange and red along with silver— reflections of the firebirds' feathers, of all the small fires now burning through the trees.

A firebird crosses the disco ball's path and hovers there, mesmerized by the shine.

Sae aims.

Poof!

Marilla whoops again, this time for me. "You're really hypnotizing the firebirds! Keep playing!"

Before playing the next notes, I aim my clarinet where most of the firebirds have gathered. A disco ball-sized silver image forms at the end of my clarinet and heads straight for them. Sae lets go of their arrow.

Poof!

I grin around the mouthpiece of my clarinet, unable to

keep my giddiness away. Maybe I *will* be okay with whatever weapon's waiting for me at the top of Kunlun Mountain. Maybe I won't fail again.

I play, silver emerges, and it's Erlang's turn. *Goodbye, firebird!*

We shoot down a few more firebirds before my asthma catches up with me. I ignored the heat and smoke and now there's a whistling sound coming out of my throat (the kind where even if I used my rescue inhaler, I'd still be breathless for a bit). My eyes sting with smoke as the realm keeps burning. And Sae and Erlang are still trying to shoot down Chaos's last sun. It's the fastest of the firebirds and the smallest, proving the hardest to catch.

"Just one more note, Astrid!" Sae shouts, trying to close in on the firebird with a purple arrow.

"I'm . . . trying!" But my lungs are on empty and my old panic is back, swirling thick through me. The air's getting smokier by the second.

What if this is it? What if we don't get any further when it comes to saving the realm? What if the immortal peaches are going to be gone forever?

I breathe in as deep as I can and force out one final note. The silvery image it shapes is tiny, its shine flickering as though it's nearly out of batteries. The bit of silver barely lifts off before it simply fades away.

It seems an eternity later when Erlang finally manages to aim true, and his golden arrow turns the last firebird into a puff of smoke.

Almost instantly, the cracks in the ground begin to close up, the soil softens and grows rich again, and all the fires start to go out. The sky blazes an early morning blue, clearer than ever. We all stand there for a moment, as if in a trance.

Marilla snaps out of it first and races up to me. "That was *awesome*. You totally helped!"

"Until the end."

She shrugs. "That's why Sae and Erlang are here. Just remember to use your inhaler ahead of time and it'll be fine."

Erlang rests a hand on my shoulder. "You did well, Astrid."

"Next time, you'll do even better," Sae adds.

I really hope they're right. What if I never again figure out how to balance air and playing? I cough out the last of the heat. Well, at least we've beaten Chaos—for now.

Sae's bow and arrow change back to their straw basket full of flowers and plants, Erlang's back to his triple-pointed spear. After I take a puff from my rescue inhaler, I start taking apart my clarinet, putting each piece back into its slot in the case. But when I go to change the reed,

I discover I can't—I forgot to refill the container after Friday's class! (To be fair, we were barely home before ending up in Zhen.) That means I'm on my very last reed. I'll have to be careful, or no more clarinet playing.

My foot kicks at something on the ground. It's a bright red rock, slightly curved. I pick it up, nearly dropping it in surprise at its warmth, at its deep smoky scent.

Not a rock—a claw from a fallen firebird.

"Gross," Marilla says from high up on Erlang's shoulder. "Are you going to keep it?"

Gross, sure, but also a cool souvenir. Libby and Jasper will get a kick out of it when I show them. When I tell them how the earth came *this* close to burning up!

"Yup, totally keeping it." I let Howl sniff it a few times before I zip it into my backpack. Just then my stomach growls, loudly enough for everyone to hear.

Sae grins. "I think it's time for some food."

• • •

Breakfast turns out to be magic—literally.

Sorting through their basket, Sae sets aside petals and leaves and bits of grass. They use their hoe to dig these into the ground and then the flat part of the tool to tamp it all down.

A moment later, plants begin to grow. The plants are covered in berries and nuts. Seeds and small fruits. One plant grows hollow vines fat with drinking water. Another has wide leaves that are buttery soft, smelling of honey.

"Whoa," I whisper. Dad's not into mythology like the rest of us, but he'd love this part to do with plants.

Sae picks a leaf and hands it to me. "Membao. Bread of Zhen."

I take a bite. It *tastes* like honey, too. One bite makes me realize how hungry I am, and I quickly eat the rest.

"This is the Chinese mythology version of lembas!" Marilla says, trying to paw a leaf free. I pluck it off the stem and break off bits for her. "It's from *Lord of the Rings*. It's bread where one bite can keep a grown man full for days."

Erlang feeds leaves to Howl. "Ridiculous."

Sae laughs. "Unfortunately, membao can't do that. None of this can. But magic has many ways; once we're hungry again, I only need a moment to grow more food."

Marilla tries to peek inside Sae's straw basket. "What other forms of magic are in there?"

The immortal tips it forward. "This yellow flower is for clarity, so I can communicate with gods and goddesses in the Heavens. This black sprig is geng, which instantly cures nausea. And here is a leaf from the buk fai yoo shrub—boiled into a tincture, the medicine heals bruises."

"*Neat*," she says.

After all the food's gone and everyone's full, we enter the trees once more.

"How far away is Kunlun Mountain?" I ask.

"If we keep a steady pace," Sae says, "we should get there by tomorrow afternoon."

We stay west, the sun at our backs. There's no real path or trail, and definitely nothing like a paved road. Just a wide soil-and-grass-patched landscape, with trees and bushes turning the horizon green. But it still *feels* like there's a path, like the earth itself is showing us the quickest way to the top, saying, "Hurry, hurry!"

We see more of Chaos's grim magic, too. Not just ribbons of white anymore but wide airport runways of it; not just branches but full shrubs. We walk through a sleeping grove of huge trees and it's like being caught in the middle of winter. A stream trickles by and all the sleeping fish inside float along instead of swim.

At one point we pass by peaks of tiled roofs, poking out from inside the trees.

"Houses!" Marilla shouts from Howl's back. "Do mortals live there?"

"They do," Erlang says.

"Why isn't there anyone around?"

"Before the Jade Emperor fell under Chaos's spell, he managed to send out warning messages to Zhen's mortals via a fleet of royal bees. They all went into hiding, thinking it would make a difference. Now they're also asleep, waiting for us to wake them up."

"It's like 'Sleeping Beauty.' When the whole kingdom is put under a spell and needs to be saved by the prince."

Erlang lifts a brow. "Were there no actual *warriors* around to do the saving?"

"I don't know. But 'Sleeping Beauty' isn't a story about warriors, anyway."

"Were princesses not allowed to do the saving, then? Zhen has many capable princesses."

"I guess princes always got first dibs. It's a really old-fashioned fairy tale. Mom says they don't write them like that anymore."

"I should think not."

The sun's high in the sky by now, a yellow blob just like the sun back home. If you ignore the faintest hint of smoke still in the air and skip your eyes past the tiniest cracks in the ground that still have to close up, you'd never know Chaos just tried to set the realm on fire.

Marilla jumps at moss starting to grow back. "Maybe Chaos will be scared of *us* now and will just stick to stealing qi. My track coach says mind games can make a big difference, and that it's always better if we get into our competitors' heads before they get into ours."

We have mind games for band class, too. Mrs. Battiste says that if we practice a complicated part over and over again in our heads, when we finally have to play it onstage for real, our minds are tricked into thinking we've already done it, so it feels less hard. I tried it for Winter Fest and it didn't work at all.

"I don't know if Chaos is going to fall for any mind games," I say, "just like I don't think we'll fall for any of his. He tried to scare us with Hou Yi's suns, but we're still going to Kunlun Mountain. I have to stop the prophecy somehow, but he also has to make it come true. We're all even steven."

Sae smiles. "You have become each other's balance. It's in Chaos's nature to destroy and in yours to bring order."

"Like yin and yang!" Marilla exclaims. "When our own is in balance, that's when we're strongest. And when things in nature are in balance, that's the true flow of the universe."

"Yin and yang *is* a special balance of two elements, yes. Not opposites, but rather that one exists because the other does. For example, it takes daylight to show you what darkness is, and sadness to understand joy. Order exists because chaos does."

"Like the myth of Pangu," I say, thinking of our

painting at home. "How the universe was once all chaos, and then order formed out of it, and that's the universe today."

Erlang nods. "Except now Chaos has been reborn, and he wants to rewrite it so that in the end, it's order that loses."

By beating me.

I touch white-as-bone shrubs as I pass, and that menacing feeling as Chaos loomed overhead runs through me again, making me shudder. It really *is* a good plan to steal a peach ahead of time, just in case.

We keep going, only stopping to grow lunch. Erlang grumbles about the time it'll take.

"But you're a demigod," I say. "Doesn't the mortal half of you still need to eat?"

"Indeed not." He flashes a smug grin. "My god half makes up for that weakness."

Sae finishes digging bits of plants into the ground. "What Erlang means is that while divine beings don't need food the same way mortals do, we still like to eat. Just as we sometimes like to sleep."

Marilla narrows her cat eyes at the warrior. "You definitely ate a ton of membao this morning. And you snore even louder than Howl."

Erlang hmphs. "None of that changes the fact that if

not for your mortal needs, we would be able to travel at night. More than that, if not for your mortal weight, we'd have called the clouds by now."

My stomach sinks. How did I forget that divine beings can travel by cloud? Some of Mom's paintings even show gods and goddesses standing on fluffy white clouds in the sky (though, when I was really little, I thought everyone just liked hanging out up there). Sae, Erlang, and Howl must have traveled that way out to the field where they first found us.

No wonder Erlang's annoyed at all the delays. If it wasn't a weak mortal who happened to find the Scroll of Chaos, Zhen might already be saved by now.

"We promise to barely slow you down." I try to think of something else positive to say. "Um, sleep's actually kind of overrated." Not true. "And humans can go for days without eating, you know." Ha-ha.

"Don't worry about things that can't be helped," Sae says. Plants bloom out of the ground and we all start picking food from their stems. "We still have more than enough time to reach the top of the mountain before the demon is too strong to stop."

"No thanks to you two," Erlang mutters.

Marilla leaps onto his cape, climbs up to his shoulder, and digs her claws in.

"Hey!" he says.

"Listen, *demi*god," she says. "Mortals can be great, too, you know. Even if we do need to eat and sleep and can't float around on clouds."

I know where this is going. I just eat membao and wait.

"For example," my sister continues, "the Chinese legend Bruce Lee was once just as powerful as you. Back when he was alive."

Erlang scowls. He tosses Howl some membao. "Who is this 'Bruce Lee,' anyway? Is he a god of some kind in your realm?"

"Hero, not god. And he was a kung fu master. I was using his moves when I first attacked you as a cat, remember my kick? I learned a lot about qi and yin and yang from him. He also talked about life energy all the time! He talked about being like water and—"

"Wait!" I blurt out. *Water!* "Why don't we travel by water?" That would definitely be faster than walking. "There must be rivers between here and Kunlun Mountain, right? It could be just like 'The Eight Immortals Cross the Sea.'"

Marilla's ears flick back and forth, thinking, then she turns her attention to Sae. "Is that the myth when you change your straw basket into a boat?"

The immortal smiles, but it doesn't reach their eyes.

The look in them says Sae's scared of something, something that's not even Chaos.

I remember them waking up from a nightmare.

The water! they shouted.

"It is that myth," Sae says, "but there's more to 'The
Eight Immortals Cross the Sea' than you know."

TEN

"What do you mean?" I ask. "Like a secret part that never reached our realm for some reason?"

"Not exactly," Sae says. "Do you remember how the myth ends?"

I'm about to say yes when Marilla admits, "Not really. Can you tell it again right now?"

"Oh, it's in the handbook!" I take it out of my bag and flip to the right page. Walking at the same time, I start to read:

The Eight Immortals Cross the Sea

Xiwangmu, Queen Mother of the West, decided to have a banquet one year, celebrating the fruits and flowers of her beautiful garden. She invited all her closest friends, and these included the Eight Immortals. They were the most beloved beings in the realm, for once they had been mortals, and only by having true goodness in their hearts did Xiwangmu gift them with immortality.

At the end of the party, instead of floating home by cloud as they normally would, the immortals decided to show off their powers by traveling home by sea.

Han Xiangze floated on top of his flute.

Zhang Guolao's donkey swam him through the water.

Lu Dongbin stood on his sword like it was a surfboard.

Li Tieguai's iron crutch turned into a piece of wood.

Quan Zhongli's fan became a small boat.

Cao Guojiu's jade imperial tablet changed into a raft.

He Xiangu's lotus flower floated out onto the water like a bed.

And as for Lan Caihe, their straw basket stretched out into a raft, and Lan Caihe sat down inside, their treasured jade clappers and magical flowers tucked into their lap.

The group of friends began to cross the East Sea, still laughing from the party. And in his palace beneath the water, the Dragon King grew annoyed at the laughter. He sent his son, the Dragon Prince, above to the surface to get rid of the loud immortals.

But when the Dragon Prince (who was not only spoiled but also had no talent for music at all) caught sight of Lan Caihe's beautiful jade clappers, he decided they would be his. He called for his father's royal army of shrimp soldiers and crab generals. At his command, they created waves to topple Lan Caihe into the sea.

Down they fell, all the way down to the palace at the bottom of the sea. There, the Dragon Prince took Lan Caihe's jade clappers and imprisoned the immortal.

The other immortals dove down to save their friend, and the army followed them. But the immortals fought them together by combining their own special powers.

Han Xiangzi played enchanting music on his flute to distract the soldiers from their orders.

Zhang Guolao rode his donkey through the halls, searching for Lan Caihe.

Each stroke of Lu Dongbin's sword was a soldier's terrible end.

Li Tieguai released a sleep potion from his medicine-filled gourd, putting generals to sleep.

Quan Zhongli used his great fan as a spear.

Cao Guojiu's jade tablet learned to smash.

And He Xiangu shook her lotus flower, the petals becoming blades as they flew through the air.

Furious, the Dragon King called the rest of the Dragon Kings from around the realm to help him. They were his brothers and were the Dragon Kings of the West, South, and North Seas. Each king brought in their own army, and soon a huge war erupted.

The fighting created a tsunami that roared through the East Sea. When the realm's mountains began to fall, the Jade Emperor ordered an end to the war. And so, the Dragon Prince had to release Lan Caihe and give back the jade clappers.

Reunited, the Eight Immortals happily continued home,

realizing that despite their different abilities, by working together, many goals could be achieved.

Reaching the end of the story, I shut the book and slide it into the outer pocket of my backpack.

"So, the immortals *didn't* happily make their way home?" I ask, really hoping I'm wrong. Maybe the rest of the myth got lost between this realm and ours. Just like no one at home knows about the Scroll of Chaos.

Sae shakes their head. "We did celebrate the whole journey back to our home island. I was saved and my friends were relieved. That's how the myth ends in your realm and how the myth ends here in Zhen, too. But that's not how it ends for me."

"What do you mean?"

"I can't travel by water anymore." Their eyes are far away. "I'm scared of something happening again and that the next time, I'll stay stuck below. The other immortals are understanding, but I know they're also impatient for me to voyage with them again . . ."

Trapped. Maybe close to how Mom feels when the fog in her head is thickest.

"The Dragon Prince doesn't deserve *any* clappers for himself." Marilla's tail whips furiously through the tall grass at our feet.

Erlang grunts and shoves fruit into his mouth. After eating our fill at the site of the plants, we picked off the rest of the food to carry with us. "I've never much enjoyed battling him or the king. Their thoughts have grown as slippery as the sea they live beneath."

Sae digs in their basket and takes out their famous clappers. Joined at the top with a string, the rectangular pieces of jade are bigger than I thought they would be. The green color of the stone gleams beneath the sunlight, rich and lustrous.

No wonder the Dragon Prince wanted them. Maybe he thought they were so beautiful that just having them would finally let him be able to play. (A small part of me understands this. I'd love to always be able to play my clarinet perfectly. To always be able to breathe and be strong and never have to worry about messing up again.) Or maybe the Dragon Prince is just as spoiled as the myth says.

Sae plays a few notes, clapping the pieces of jade together with their hands. Deep and melodious *gongs* chime into the air. "Sometimes I wish the prince had just kept them," they confess. "Because I see them and hold them and remember all over again how scared I was that day. But then I play again and I'm glad they're still mine."

"One day, Sae," Erlang says, "you will no longer be scared of the water."

Sae puts their clappers back into their basket. "One day."

I really hope Erlang's right. Sae hating to be in deep water just as Chaos plans to flood Zhen is pretty much the World's Worst Combo. Or maybe it's Second Worst, when I think about how I have to fight the demon. I mean, what kind of realm-saving hero has asthma, anyway?

Howl suddenly barks and takes off, disappearing into the nearby trees. Ten seconds later, he comes back, still barking.

Marilla stops walking. "He smells something," she says. The fur on her back lifts. "Something not good."

"He smells the Moving Sands," Erlang says. The way his expression changes isn't a good one, and a knot forms inside my gut.

Howl runs off again, continuing to bark.

"Howl!" Erlang commands, then stomps after his dog, still calling.

Sae runs by, too. "Come—this is the route to Kunlun Mountain, there's no avoiding it."

The Moving Sands. Even the name sounds creepy. Like something alive.

"Why does that name sound familiar?" I say to Marilla. "Is it a myth Mom used to tell us?"

"I don't know. But let's go. I don't like it here by ourselves."

"Maybe I saw it in here . . ." I murmur, grabbing *A Handbook of Ancient Chinese Myths* from my backpack pocket and flipping the pages. "Here it is!" It's one of the myths that's only as long as a couple of sentences:

The Moving Sands

The Moving Sands is one of the great obstacles to Kunlun Mountain. Outside of Chinese mythology, it is known more commonly as quicksand.

"Uh, I don't think I wanted to know that," my sister says. Her fur stays ruffled. "Everything I know about quicksand comes from movies where every character screams about it being dangerous."

"Same here." But then I grin. "But you know what? Jasper watched all those old *Mythbusters* episodes, and there was one on quicksand. He said science proves no one actually sinks! It's denser than water, so we'd just float on top." I zip the book into my backpack to keep it sand free.

"We just . . . lie flat on our backs, then? Like we were in a pool?"

"Sure." Jasper didn't say this part was in *Mythbusters*,

but since we float even in water, it makes sense to me.

Marilla looks doubtful. "But this is Zhen quicksand. It might not follow the same rules."

"I guess there's only one way to find out."

We run after the others. I get peeks of them through the trees, like crumbs laid out along a path—blue silk, gold armor, gray fur.

"It might just be a small patch," Marilla says. "That we can just, you know, hop over?"

I huff. "It said *obstacle*, though."

"You know, I'm pretty sure I remember one movie where the bad guy died in quicksand—not because they sank, but because they got stuck and couldn't get out."

I never thought about that. "We're not going to get stuck."

"But—"

"Let's not worry about it until we have to, okay?" I sound cross, when I'm just scared.

"Sure, sorry."

I focus on keeping my breathing even. We both stare down at the ground as we run, as though any second hard dirt might change into deathly sand.

The woods start to open up. The trees fall away to reveal Sae and Erlang and Howl, standing and looking out at something. Marilla and I come to a stop beside them as the sun flashes off the biggest desert I've ever seen.

The Moving Sands.

The quicksand seems to go on forever. This huge brown nothingness that stretches out so far it even pushes the horizon away, making the rest of the realm seem to disappear. There's no breeze, as not a single grain of sand moves. The surface is also completely flat. Nothing like the deserts back home, full of dunes and swells and hollows.

Staring at the strange flatness, there's something almost inviting about it. The way you want to cut into a perfectly iced cake. How fresh snow practically begs you to be the first to run through it. Once when the school parking lot was getting repaved, so many kids couldn't resist sneaking in their shoeprints that we all got detention. Libby said it was worth it if it meant becoming immortal in a way.

But no parking lot or snow or cake ever screamed danger like this.

The cold knot in my gut spreads out into a panicky storm. There's no way we can cross this without sinking. This is as far as we go.

"Astrid."

I turn. Sae's expression is nothing but chill, telling me to be chill, too. "You know what I think? The prophecy wouldn't have said it could be stopped if it was already decided we would lose."

Hope peeks through the swirling panic. "You think so?"

They smile. "Of course, we still have to figure out how we're going to cross."

Marilla dares to knock at some grains with her paw. "Even if we do figure it out, it'll probably take us all day to get across. Maybe even days."

And to walk around the entire desert would take . . . I can't even guess, that's how big it feels. Whatever the answer might be, it's still too long.

Erlang sighs in exasperation. "Listen, mortals, it shouldn't be *that* hard to cross the Moving Sands. It's really just a simple matter of allowing the surface to adjust to our weight between each movement."

My sister's ears flick. "How do you know that?"

"Because there are stories over the centuries of both mortals *and* higher beings who managed to cross. It seems magic isn't the key but merely strategy."

"When *does* magic work?" I ask.

"It works until it doesn't." Erlang squints across the sand. "But I say we take our chances and try with magic first. It's faster."

"Sae, your straw basket!" I say. "You can blow it up like a raft and we can use it to cross the Moving Sands!"

"Good idea." The immortal sifts through their basket, moving blossoms and small plants aside. Soon they pull out a tiny seedling of a plant.

"Fee-neh herb," they tell us. "A few of the leaves expand my basket so I can sit inside. But to fit the four of us . . ." They crush the entire seedling in their hands, press their palms against the basket, and set it down on the ground.

The basket creaks and cracks. It grows until it's the size of a tiny lifeboat.

Sae leans over to gather the flowers still in the basket's bottom. They tuck them into a pocket of their silk robe and then pick up their hoe. "All magic has a breaking point, so let's hope we're far from it yet. Hop in."

Marilla leaps in first, followed by Howl. Then it's Sae and then me. Erlang nudges the basket toward the sand with his foot. It starts to coast forward and he hops inside the basket before it's out of reach.

We slide onto the Moving Sands.

For a second, everyone freezes, not even daring to breathe, as though the quicksand has a mind of its own and is listening for trespassers, wanting to swallow us up as soon as it can. But nothing happens. The sand doesn't immediately collapse so that we fall in. No Dragon Prince popping up from the liquid beneath, either, screaming at Sae for their clappers.

The basket slowly glides to a stop and we float there on the surface, the same way a real raft sits on water.

"Now what?" Marilla whispers.

"Now we cross." Erlang drops his spear over the side of the basket and begins to use it like an oar through the sand. Sae does the same with their hoe on the opposite side.

The basket begins moving once more.

I peer over the edge. Brown sand whisks by, the basket's bottom riding the current being stirred up by Sae and Erlang's rowing. I think of how Marilla and I used to bury each other in beach sand, all the way up to our necks, because it was always just sand. We could get out whenever we wanted.

"It'll be sunset before we reach the other side." Sae sounds resigned. "If Zhongli were here, we'd have a great wind that would carry us right across."

Quan Zhongli is one of the Eight Immortals, the one whose fan could bring back the dead with a single wave. Using it for wind would have to be way easier.

Marilla climbs onto Erlang's shoulder and peers out across the sand. "What if we call for a wind god or goddess to help us? We can use a clarity flower."

Sae shakes their head. "The wind deities are under Chaos's spell now. Dimmed from the rest of the realm."

"I could just call for one, anyway?" she says. "I can be really loud."

"Can't you just *wish* for wind," Erlang practically growls, "and do it silently in your head?"

"I *guess*, grumpy-pants."

I watch the horizon never change. In my head I keep hearing Sae say how everyone's been dimmed. The word *dimmed* makes me feel uneasy the same way *moving sands* does. Like nothing's quite right (and so nothing is qi).

"It's like being wrapped in fog, isn't it?" I say to Sae.

"Being dimmed? Yes."

"We have demons back home who do the same thing. Dimming people."

They pause rowing, then pass me something from their robe pocket. "It's hope herb. Bring it home with you."

It's a tiny branch of needles. It looks like it could be from one of the pine trees that grow all over our neighborhood. But instead of sharp and dark green, these needles are a bright yellow and soft as velvet.

"Thanks." I sniff it. The herb kind of smells like ginseng but also different. Something brand-new. I carefully tuck the tiny branch into one of the interior pockets of my backpack, the ones no one ever really uses because they're so small (even though they also keep things safe). "How do I use it?"

Sae smiles and goes back to rowing. "Simply keep it nearby."

I lean over and let my fingers touch the sand. It feels just like that—plain old sand. I let my hand drop into it next. I push until it reaches my elbow. I begin to row, same as Sae and Erlang, wanting to move faster. The other side is still so far.

That's when a huge *craaaack* bursts through the air.

We all stop rowing and look at one another.

"What was that?" I grab the edge of the basket and look down at the sand.

The surface is as smooth as ever. Nothing looks different at all. Which doesn't explain why suddenly my stomach is churning.

Creeeaaak.

Howl barks sharply, just once, not liking the noise, either.

Erlang frowns. He stops rowing and lifts his spear back into the basket. "Hmm."

Snap!

Along the edge of the basket, my hands start sliding together, all on their own. As though I'm losing room to hold on.

"Oh," Sae whispers. They pull their hoe out of the sand and set it back on their shoulder. "That's the sound of my basket shrinking. I must have grown my basket too large and for too long."

Marilla dives back into Erlang's hood.

"Is it the Moving Sands doing it?" I ask, that earlier storm of panic back again. Everyone's knees smash together as the room inside the basket grows smaller and smaller. "The way it doesn't always let magic work here?"

"No, I think it's me," Sae says. "I don't sense my magic pushing back, so it's not this place. But my magic still feels different. Not just stretched but *shallow*." Their face pales. "It's my qi. It's Chaos."

The panic goes icy. Sae *and* Erlang are growing weaker now. (I bet Howl is, too, if he could tell me.) Just like that, Chaos's menacing presence roars back, feeling even stronger now. Closer, too, as though he's somewhere watching this. I'd probably feel sick if I wasn't already so worried about falling into quicksand. I look up at the sky for signs of a coming windstorm, but there's nothing.

Marilla wraps her paws around Erlang's neck. "*We're going to sink!*"

"It's all right, stay calm," the warrior says, trying to pry Marilla's claws free. "Panic will only make you struggle and then you *will* sink."

I let go of the basket—it's too tiny to hold on to anymore. "The basket's going to fall apart!"

"No, it will never break," Sae says. "But it *will* squeeze us out once it's small enough—better that we do it ourselves so we can control how we land."

We climb out of the basket as carefully as we can to stand on the sand's surface. The basket finishes shrinking back to its regular size and Sae picks it up.

Beneath my shoes the sand stays solid. I take a small step, careful to land softly. Then another. The others start doing it, too.

"Remember—move slowly," Erlang says. Howl stays at his side as Marilla peeks out from the folds of his cape. "Make sure the sand can hold your weight before taking the next step."

Sae groans. "At this rate we won't finish crossing until after dark. Should I grow my basket again, even if it won't last?"

"Too risky. We were lucky to get out safely even this time."

"But we need to hurry, it's—"

The ground in front of me suddenly dips and sways.

I go still, my foot in midair, breath catching in my throat. A spot on the ground beside me shifts. Sand on the surface tumbles and spins.

"Something's happening," I say, and I hear the shaking in my voice. "The ground is starting to fall in! No one move!"

Everyone freezes as more of the ground begins to roll and twist. Like the waves of the ocean, but with sand instead of water. Sand flies into the air and swirls wildly.

"It's not the ground," Sae says. Their eyes darken as they stare out across the Moving Sands. "It's Chaos. He's in the sand!"

As we watch, huge swaths of the sand around us turn bone white. It's like watching a time-lapse video of walls being painted. A deep and ugly swooshing sound begins to fill the world, and I stare up at the sky once more, fresh fear stuck in my throat. Clouds are whirling, fast and thick. The windstorm of Chaos is all around us.

Before I can decide which is worse, Chaos attacking from above or from below, the ground shifts, deciding for us as we begin to sink. Sand rises to my ankles. I'm being buried at the beach again, but this time, no one's going to pull me out.

"We need to get on our backs!" I shout over the noise of the wind as Jasper talking about floating comes back to me. "We need to spread out our weight so we can float!"

We all flop onto our backs, but a second later, we sink some more.

It's not working! Zhen quicksand must be too different. Sand climbs toward my face. My heart pounds so fast and hard it's like it's moved up into my ears. I start gasping, trying not to think about running out of air and able to think only of that.

"We need another idea!" Sae yells, no longer chill at all but sounding terrified as sand wraps itself around their neck.

"Howl, hold still!" Erlang's trying to get him to stop struggling. But the dog's panicking as much as I am and he's sinking fast.

Marilla's on top of Erlang's chest, fear fluffing her tail as wide as a raccoon's. "Astrid, I'm scared!"

"I know, I am, too!" How will Mom and Dad ever know what happened to us? This can't be happening!

The ground thunders and shakes and feels like it's opening up. We sink even deeper, and as the sand rises past my chin, I take the deepest breath I can right before the world goes dark.

ELEVEN

Farther into the earth I go. Sand from above pushes me into the ground, wrapping around me like the world's thickest, heaviest blanket, and I can't breathe.

My lungs are still screaming for air when I land on my back with a thud. *Ooof!*

Then, gasping, I think: *At least we're finally done sinking.*

More thuds as the others land beside me. In the dark I hear Erlang swear in Chinese.

Marilla's eyes glow like yellow lamps. She shakes her black coat and there's the sound of sand falling to the ground. "What is this place?"

"I'm not sure." I watch the shadowy figure of Sae tip sand from their basket. "I've never heard about an underground to the Moving Sands."

"These walls are packed sand." Erlang stomps his foot on the ground as Howl (a low-to-the-ground blob) sniffs along. "More sand beneath us, but as solid as stone."

I look around, waiting for my eyes to adjust. There are some lanterns on the wall, but they're few and far between, and their light is dim. All I can tell is that we're in a single dark room with no sign of windows or doors. Instantly, my lungs want to clench up.

"We need to find a way out," I say, trying to sound calm. "The air in here won't last."

"Oh, we will." Erlang taps his knuckles along the walls. "It's just a matter of finding a weakness that we can smash through."

"No, this whole place might collapse inward," Sae says. "Don't forget, we've got the Moving Sands over our heads."

"Tell me when it's over!" Marilla squeaks. Her eyes disappear as she covers them with her paws.

I rub my eyes hard, desperate to see better. Looking around again, I notice that the darkness at the far end of the room isn't fully solid. There's something there, its edges showing up in the lantern light. Maybe it's a window or door!

"Hey, come see this!" I call out as I rush over, hands out so I don't break my nose. My fingers run into more hardened sand, and it's not the sand of the wall. With my eyes finally adjusted all the way, I step back to see what's in front of me.

It's a statue. There are two, side by side, and they're even taller than Erlang. They're also warriors of some kind, with plates of armor over their bodies and swords in their hands. Helmets come down low over their eyes like half masks. I scrape at their armor and hold the grains of sand up to a lantern—they're paler than the sandstone around the room. Whoever they'd been, the statues are now under Chaos's spell.

"There's a door behind each one!" Marilla says excitedly as she runs over to get a closer look.

Sae walks over to push one open. It doesn't budge.

"Let me try." Erlang shoves his shoulder into the door. It doesn't budge for him, either. He scowls up at it. "There's magic keeping this shut."

"It's these guards." Sae examines their swords. "They're here to watch over the doors, but grim magic has put them to sleep. If we want to leave, we have to find a way to wake them up."

"The doors have names carved above them." Marilla points with a paw. "One says *life* and the other says *death*." Her paw drops. "This seems bad."

"No, it must be a second chance after you fall through the Moving Sands!" I wonder how they decide which door you get. Imagine thinking you're okay just to find out it's all a trick. There's only one door we want.

"How are we going to wake up the guards?" Marilla asks.

Sae shakes their head. "I have no idea. If we can't figure it out, we'll just have to find another way out of here."

Erlang goes back to the door marked LIFE and starts

pushing at it again. Howl leans up and scratches at it, whining.

"I told you, it won't be that simple," Sae says, annoyed. "That's why there are guards."

Erlang steps back, scowling again, but this time at the immortal. "Do you have a better idea?"

"How to wake them up? No, otherwise I would have done it already."

"Then instead of complaining, why don't you help me open this door?"

"Why would I do that when it's clearly a waste of time and energy?"

Marilla climbs up my leg and arm to reach my ear. She whispers, "They're seriously arguing. They *never* seriously argue."

"I just hope they don't start fighting." We watch as Sae and Erlang both start pointing fingers at the doors and then at each other's faces. "Especially with real magic."

Alarm makes Marilla's tail fluff out again. "What if this is Chaos creating, you know, *chaos*? By making them fight?"

I glance around uneasily, remembering how the demon was in the sand above. "And to slow us down."

"We need to distract them. Make them forget they even argued."

And not just ignore it, like we do, I think. *So that it bothers them forever.*

"Okay, but how?" The edges of my clarinet case suddenly dig into my back. "Play my clarinet?" I ask, not really seriously.

Her cat eyes gleam. "Actually, that's such a weird idea, it might just work."

I quickly put my clarinet together and play a single E.

Instantly, Sae and Erlang stop arguing and look over. I keep playing more easy notes at random, making sure they're not about to start up again (Mom and Dad say some arguments need to run their course).

"Halt there!"

I stop playing as the statues lift their swords into the air. My clarinet nearly slips from my hand as my mouth drops open.

"Oh my gosh, you woke them up!" Marilla's claws dig into my shoulder. "With your playing!"

No way. But it's true—the sandstone of the guards is now the same shade as the rest of the room. And I wasn't even playing with yao grass, the way I did with Chaos's ten suns. It was just . . . me.

Erlang holds out his spear. "Who are you?" Beside him, Howl crouches, growling.

"Ushers for this part of the Moving Sands," the guards

say together. They sound like robots (and not nice ones). "All trespassers are required to move on. Give us gifts and we'll decide which door is to be yours."

Sae narrows their eyes. "No stories of those who successfully crossed the Moving Sands mention a pair of ushers or this underground room. Why is that?"

I feel my stomach churn as the answer suddenly dawns on all of us.

"Anyone who's ever fallen from the sands above has only ever been shown one door." They both lift their swords toward the same one.

DEATH.

"Nothing has ever been good enough?" Erlang's voice is cold, but he lowers his spear. "What kind of gifts are you looking for?"

"Something worthy of us. We are ancient, practically timeless, and we demand gifts of equal substance. Do that, and you will be shown the door to *life*." The statues swivel and lift their swords.

"Otherwise—"

"*Death*. And do not think of challenging us to a duel as an alternative," they say as Erlang's hand drops to his spear, "for you will not win. Gifts are your only way."

Erlang practically sputters. "What do you mean *not win*—"

"We understand," Sae says quickly, "and we agree. Please forgive our friend. He's a demigod—very short of temper."

Both statues lower their swords. "Then present your gift."

The rest of us exchange glances, each one trying to think of what we could possibly offer.

Sae takes out something bead-sized from their basket. "First, a seed of the—"

"No. Only your entire basket will do."

Sae pales and their hand clutches their basket tight. "But—that's not possible."

They're right, it can't be! Sae without their basket of magic wouldn't be Sae at all.

"That is the gift we demand," the statues say. "Not one bit of magic, but all."

"Impossible!" Erlang points his spear at the guards again, who immediately raise their swords in response. No one moves for several tense seconds.

I have to do something, I think. *But what?*

"I have an even better gift!" I say in a rush, before I can think about it too deeply and chicken out. "My music."

The guards turn to look at me as everyone else goes still.

"Your music?" they say in unison.

I nod, even as the pinched, breathless feeling creeps back into my chest. It's actually not as bad as it usually is since I've already played in front of Sae and Erlang. And I'll just stick to the easy notes, same as always.

"Music lasts forever because you can play it in your head over and over again, for as long as you like," I reason. "And it's very powerful music, too, since it woke you both up from Chaos's spell. If I play for you, then all of us get to leave through the *life* door."

The statues look at each other as if considering my offer, then turn back to me.

"Yes, we accept this gift. But know this: We must be completely pleased. If we are not, it will be *death*—not just for you but for your friends, too."

I swallow. Maybe I need to rethink my plan of coasting. "No do-overs?"

"None. It must be the perfect gift."

"Don't panic, you can do this," Marilla whispers before leaping off my shoulder. I nearly ask Sae for some yao grass, but the immortal is already stepping back to make room, and I swallow again as I face the guards. My chest goes even tighter as words race around in my head: *The perfect gift, or death for everyone.*

No coasting. If I somehow give away that I'm skipping over the high notes, we're all goners. How can I take that chance? I shut my eyes hard for a second, reminding myself how I've already done more here in Zhen than I ever thought I could. I helped bring down firebirds! I woke up these statues all on my own!

I take a deep breath, imagining my air sweeping the panic out of my lungs, and start playing "Path of the Wind."

At the first high note, nervousness flutters hard against my ribs. But the note holds steady, and I keep going. As I play my way to the next high note, I can tell it's already going much better than this morning when the heat and smoke and my own carelessness made my lungs go small. Every note is full and strong. I imagine Mom right here in the room with me, her eyes telling me how awesome I sound, her grin that says I've never played better.

Halfway through my solo, the air around my clarinet starts to *shimmer*.

My eyes go wide. Still somehow managing to play, I watch as the shimmer happens again, the air puckering around my clarinet like twisted cling wrap. Through the shimmer's blur, the room wavers and billows.

By the end of the song, the air's no longer moving, and everything is silent for a moment. *It's all the shadows in here,* I tell myself. *Playing tricks on me.*

I lower my clarinet and Marilla starts clapping her paws

together. Sae grins and Erlang smirks smugly at the guards. Even Howl seems pleased, tail held high.

"*Life* . . . it is," the guards declare, and the one standing in front of the LIFE door moves aside. The room shakes slightly, sand pattering down from the ceiling like rain, as the sandstone door slides open.

TWELVE

We step through and find ourselves at the bottom of a steep ravine. The bottom and sides are covered with clover, bright green and reaching up to my waist. Grim magic hasn't reached down here yet.

Howl and Marilla leap away and disappear into the green.

"Meet us at the top!" I shout at them as I start to put away my clarinet.

"That dog needs to burn off some energy in a good battle," Erlang says, stretching as though he's been cooped up for days.

"Which he might yet." Sae tilts their face to the sun. "I thought I saw enough sun this morning to last me an immortal's lifetime but apparently not."

Erlang gazes upward, too, but only to check the time. "It'll be dark in a few hours—we should go."

I take a just-in-case puff of my inhaler before I start walking up the steep ravine, Sae leading us away from the hidden underground. Clover crushes open beneath our feet and the air smells of oranges and rain. Sometimes the green plants shake as creatures run away from our feet, and I wonder how long it's been since they've been disturbed. Wherever DEATH led to, it's not here (which is awesome).

Marilla and Howl are waiting at the top. We all turn west and start walking.

Zhen on this side of the Moving Sands is a lot like the other—trees and shrubs, grass and moss and soil. But other than the bottom of the deep ravine where everything was still awake and bright green, this part of the realm is already nearly completely under Chaos's spell. Hilly meadows are beaches of white sand. Huge lots of pale gray earth. Entire forests are asleep, hundreds of trees like great spindly ghosts wearing white canopies for hair. (Once I point out a whole family of sleeping owls, fat bodies unmoving and feathers so white they seem dipped in paint. "Zhen owls are known for their bright coloring," Erlang says, sounding especially offended. "Crimson as blood, purple as violets.")

We're headed toward where Chaos is most powerful. Whatever's between here and Kunlun is going to be even worse than quicksand.

I stuff a piece of leftover membao into my mouth, wanting to fill myself up so the ugly doomed feeling that's all Chaos won't fill me up instead.

"No reason to be scared, Astrid." Erlang taps his gold

(and now smudged) chest armor. "You and your sister are traveling in my company, a hero's. I'm a demigod trusted to fight for divine rulers and to defend entire realms; I won't let you mortals down."

Erlang might be mostly right about mortals being weaker, but I really need him to be wrong soon. Because in the end, I'm still the one who has to beat Chaos. Just me and no one else. Astrid Xu, one hundred percent mortal.

Ugh. I shove more membao in my mouth and try not to think about it anymore. I toss some bread to Howl, who happily wolfs it down (he and Bear would be good friends).

"Well, Bruce Lee was a hero *and* mortal," Marilla says, back onto one of her favorite subjects. "He didn't save people's lives or anything, but he was still a hero to Chinese people by becoming a kung fu master in Hollywood."

"And 'Hollywood' is?" Sae asks.

"A place where people make up stories. Except they call the stories movies."

Erlang's expression turns thoughtful. "If he didn't save lives, then how does becoming this 'kung fu master' in movies make him a hero?"

"Because he made Hollywood see how boring their movies were without him. He made other Chinese people realize how cool they already were, even if no one else thought so."

Mom and Dad told my sister this information ages ago. If Bruce Lee was a subject in school, she'd ace every single test.

Erlang nods. "It's clear you've chosen a worthy leader in your Bruce Lee, Marilla. I should remember that mortals can be just as capable of great things, as my father was both a gifted scholar and guardian of our family. It's actually because of him that I became strong in the first place."

"How?" I ask. I don't know much about Erlang's dad. Myths don't talk a lot about mortals.

"Before he died, he made sure I would always take care of my mother. When I was a teenager and she was imprisoned inside Mount Hua, I had to learn how to use my spear to break apart the mountain in order to rescue her." Erlang sighs. "Except now my truth-seeing eye is starting to fail, and I feel once again like a boy, starting from the very beginning. I'm worried I won't be able to rescue her again."

Sae's right—between nightmares and moms needing to be saved, immortals aren't that different from us.

"She's also at the palace?" I ask. Erlang might be the strongest warrior in Chinese mythology, but I still wish I could make him feel better.

"She is." Erlang grimaces. "And not only is my eye growing weaker, it's also starting to tell me lies instead of truth. Until soon I will doubt my own mind."

Sae looks troubled. "What kind of lies?"

"That I never rescued my mother at all and she's been imprisoned inside Mount Hua this entire time. That I've already failed to rescue her now and she will never be freed of grim magic."

"You should have told me," Sae says quietly. "You know I understand how fears can live in your head. I would have told you what was true and what wasn't."

"I know you would have. But it'll just keep happening until Chaos is stopped. This is why I must see Astrid to the top of Kunlun." He glowers at some nearby trees like they're Chaos himself. "Not only to rescue my mother and the rest of the realm, but because I'm scared that I'll never be strong again."

"You'll still always be Erlang Shen, super warrior," I say.

"Warriors are not weak."

"You'd just be strong in a different way. Like how your dad was a mortal but still strong, right?"

He just grunts, still glowering (but now at different trees).

"But it doesn't matter, because I know you'll get to rescue your mom." Just like how I know Mom's going to be saved, too.

Erlang finally nods, then gives a hard grin. "Demon-destroying time—I'm looking forward to it."

As he goes to throw a stick into the trees for Howl to fetch, Marilla climbs onto my shoulder. "Erlang's so cool," she whispers into my ear. "Nearly as cool as Bruce Lee!"

• • •

The sun is nearly all the way down, the realm tinged with red and shadows everywhere.

Sae points to a clump of trees up ahead. "That's where we'll set up for the night."

Marilla and Howl run ahead.

"Are we getting close enough to see Kunlun Mountain soon?" I ask. At home you can see the local ski mountains even from far away. But here the horizon stays perfectly flat, with no sign of the mountain. I've been checking all day. It's hard to feel excited about meeting Chaos face-to-face, but seeing Kunlun in person is another story. "Mom, it's real!" is how I'll start.

"We'd see it tomorrow if not for the divine cloud cover that keeps it hidden from this distance," Erlang says. "I'd like to promise that my third eye will still be able to see it, but I cannot."

Sae pokes through their basket for the plants to grow dinner. "We'll reach the Red River first. Its waters fuel this part of Zhen, and its source is Kunlun. Our route will be as simple as following the line of the river."

"That's it?" I ask. "Just the river is left?"

Erlang looks up from brushing dirt off his helmet's plume. "Well, there's—"

Sae exchanges a quick glance with him before going back to their basket. "Yes, just the river."

Erlang nods and keeps brushing off his plume. "You can already hear it, now that the noise of day is past."

We go quiet, and just like that, the sound of the river comes. It's a fat hum in the background, the kind that disappears once you forget to listen for it. I never notice how loud the fridge is until the power goes out.

"It sounds so close," I say.

"Just past the next few stands of trees." Sae digs blossoms and leaves into the ground with their hoe. Marilla and Howl race back in time to see dinner sprout up.

"Uh-oh," Marilla says. "I don't think there's as many berries and fruits on these plants as before."

She's right. And while the new membao plant is still full, its soft bread-like leaves are already drooping. Their honey scent swirling into the air is faint.

Sae pulls a blossom at random from their basket—its once-blue petals are mostly white. Whatever magic it held is nearly completely gone. Sae probably wouldn't even be able to grow their basket now.

"What if you and Erlang fall under his spell before we get to Kunlun Mountain?" My eyes are stuck on the sleeping flower. I can't imagine Marilla and me trying to get the rest of the way alone. (We're not even allowed to take the city bus by ourselves.) Not to mention I still don't know what kind of weapon is hidden in the parasol trees. What if I can't figure out how to use it?

Sae drops the blossom back into their basket. "We won't. I promise."

"Howl knows the way, just in case?" Marilla asks.

"He does," Erlang says. Howl barks once.

"And then Astrid will go all Bruce Lee on Chaos." My sister kicks the air. "Right, Astrid?"

"Right." I can't tell her that she could teach me all of Bruce Lee's signature moves and I still won't be sure. I helped shoot down Chaos's suns but ran out of air when it mattered.

While the membao doesn't taste bad (but definitely nothing like honey), no one seems to want too much of it. But the berries and nuts and seeds still taste good, so Sae grows a couple more plants' worth, and we mostly fill up on those. I save the rest of the membao for later, just in case.

"I have to pee," Marilla whispers to me as I zip up my backpack. It's the deal we made—whenever it's dark out, I have to go with her.

Marilla and I head deeper into the trees. I count steps (human ones, not cat) as we walk.

"Fifty?" my sister asks.

"Fifty." Just far enough from camp for privacy. "Now ten more in opposite directions."

"I have to go number two."

That means an extra ten steps. We both count to twenty out loud and then turn our backs to each other.

I'm done before Marilla is, and she comes bounding out of the trees. "I can't believe how used I am to moving like a cat now. It's honestly so much fast—"

I crouch down to cat level. "If I tell you something, will you promise not to tell Sae and Erlang?"

Marilla's ears flick back and forth. I get why she's wondering about this—she likes them as much as I do. Especially Erlang. Her deciding he was nearly as cool as Bruce Lee is basically a once-in-a-lifetime event.

"What can't we tell them?" she asks.

"It's about how we want to get an immortal peach for Mom. I was thinking—what if the Queen Mother of the West says no?"

"Why would she say no? You're saving the realm."

"Because I was the one who put the realm in danger in the first place. I just don't think she'll want to reward me for that."

"But . . . even if she does say no, what can we do?"

"I have a plan. Once we get to Kunlun Mountain, I'll sneak into her garden and steal a peach. That way, even if she says no, we'll already have one."

"*What?*" Her tiny cat teeth show as her mouth drops open. "No way! Don't you remember what happened to Chang'e after she stole the immortality elixir? And then there's the Monkey King getting buried! You *can't* steal from Xiwangmu!"

"You still remember their stories?" Sometimes it seems Marilla's *trying* to forget mythology, same as how she tries to forget about Mom being sick, so that we don't talk about either anymore.

Her ears flatten and her yellow-lamp eyes go narrow. "Why do you always act like you know more about mythology than I do? It's annoying."

"Because I *do* know more. Especially now."

"Nope, you don't. If you did, you'd already know that this is a really bad plan and you're going to get in so much trouble!"

"Listen, the Queen Mother's under Chaos's spell, so she won't even know until we're back home with the peach and Mom's all better. Isn't that what you want, too? Mom better?"

The fur on my sister's back stands up. "I *do* want Mom

better! But I want to do it the right way. Not doing things like making offerings to the Kitchen God, or stealing from queens who'll punish us!"

"What's the right way when nothing's worked so far?"

"*Real* ways, like actual doctors and medicine. Sure, magic made me a cat, but that was the emperor, not us. We're only going to mess up how she's *supposed* to get better because we don't know anything. We're just kids and we need to leave it alone before we get in the way. Or even make things worse."

I glare at her. We've never had this argument about peaches before, but it sure feels like we have. I should have known Marilla wouldn't like my plan, since it means actually doing something. "You're just acting like you're being like water because it's a way for you to ignore Mom. But the truth is that you're scared, like always. When I bring home the peach, I'll tell Mom you didn't want me to do it!"

"I bet it won't even work!" she yells.

"Zhen magic can stop time back home—of course the peach is going to work there, too." Why can't she see she doesn't have to be scared anymore? How this is our best chance and that I can make it work?

"That's exactly why I don't want you to do it!" Marilla's voice cracks. "If you bring it back and even magic doesn't make Mom better, then . . . that's it. There's nothing else anyone can do." Her cat eyes are too shiny.

I'm confused. "But I thought you *wanted* to ask the Queen Mother for a peach."

"I *do!*" Her tail whips furiously back and forth. "Because you saving the realm and getting rewarded is how it's supposed to happen. *That's* the flow of the universe. You can't cheat by stealing."

"What matters is that we get the peach, not how—"

"I'll tell Sae and Erlang."

I stop. Grow cold all over even though it's still warm out. Would she really do that? When she's always kept my secrets? I bet she won't. She might stay angry with me for a long time afterward, but once Mom's better for real, we'll be fine again. Xu Glue sisters once more.

"I mean it. If you steal it, I really will tell." Her voice cracks again. The only sign she's as upset as she is mad.

"Fine. It was just an idea, anyway." My heart squeezes. I didn't know how much I wanted to do this together. After I do it on my own, maybe then she'll finally understand. Maybe then she'll know what it's like to hurt, too, that I don't need her after all. "Not my fault that you don't want Mom better as much as I do."

Marilla goes dead still. For a second, I think she's going to attack me with her claws (a part of me knows I deserve it), but she only snarls instead. She spins around and races away into the dark, back to camp. If my sister's fast as a human kid, she's even faster as a cat, and there's no way I can catch up. Even if I want to, which I don't. And even if *she* wants me to (which she doesn't), because she knows I can't run like that. That I never could.

THIRTEEN

I wait a minute before following her so that by the time I get back to the others, I'm less shaky. Erlang's already asleep, and Howl's sprawled out next to him. Beside Howl is Marilla, a curled-up ball of fluff. I doubt she's asleep, but I don't say anything to her. We do this at home, too, if we're still mad at each other by bedtime. Then in the morning, we just pretend we didn't even argue. I don't know if that's going to happen this time. Somehow, an argument about peaches is the worst argument we've had in a long time. Maybe ever.

Sae's still awake, though. They're sitting cross-legged in front of their tree, waving the Scroll of Chaos in the air like it's a fan.

I plop down in front of the tree beside them and dig out my medicine pouch from my backpack. I take two puffs from my regular inhaler and zip it all away again.

"Your asthma?" Sae asks in a near whisper.

I nod. "Just everyday medicine," I whisper back. I point to the scroll that they're still waving around. "What are you doing?"

"Applying a coating of gum seed extract. We use it on cuts and scratches here, but it also works as a protectant. The Jade Emperor will want the scroll back once the prophecy has been stopped."

"You must be pretty sure I'm going to beat Chaos."

"I have to be. I don't want to meet the emperor in Diyu afterward; the realm of the afterlife wouldn't be pleasing." Sae studies me. "And yourself?"

I remember how at dinner I acted like I was sure. Fake it until you make it, right? "Sometimes I'm sure. But sometimes I'm afraid. I think I feel like how Erlang feels, how he wants to save his mom but he's worried about turning weak when it counts."

"It's all right to be afraid. Fear is why there is such a thing as bravery."

"What if I try and Chaos still wins?"

"The things we want the most are also the things that scare us—all we can do is try, anyway."

I pull my knees to my chest. "Well, I wish I knew exactly how to stop the prophecy. Then I could just do it and Chaos would be destroyed."

"As rivers must flow, so does the way of the universe. Everything will make its own way."

I sigh. "Which still means all I can do is try, like you said. I guess you don't believe in the idea of fate."

Sae grins. "Fate is merely something that happens as you live it."

Erlang clears his throat. "Dawn," he says from beneath his cape that's tossed over his head. "We leave at dawn."

Sae laughs quietly, then puts the scroll away. "He's right, we should get some sleep." They settle against their tree and tuck their hands into the sleeves of their silk robe. "Does any of that help?" they whisper.

"Yeah." I like Sae's idea of what fate means. As though nothing is impossible.

"I'm glad." Sae shuts their eyes. "Good night."

"Good night." Using my backpack as a pillow, I fall asleep in seconds.

It feels like only minutes later that someone's shaking my shoulder.

"Wake up!"

I keep my eyes shut. I guess Marilla's not so mad at me that she'll go pee by herself. "Marilla, can't you just go behind a tree or something?"

"It's me, Astrid. It's Mom."

Instantly I wake up, my eyes popping open. I see darkness, the sky, and stars.

And Mom.

A warm feeling fills my chest. It's solid and comfy. It's the very opposite of how panic and worry feel when they're in there instead, taking all my air.

"Mom!" I sit up fast and hug her. She even smells right—not like she's been in bed all day but of freshly cooked rice and perfume and soap. She's wearing my favorite shirt of hers, too, a blouse with pale gray elephants all over it. She only wears it on the days she's feeling especially happy.

My mind whirls—how can she even be here? The Jade Emperor is under a spell, and Mom wouldn't have a dragon scale.

Who cares! I yell at myself. *Mom's here and she's actually better!*

Mom lets go to look at me. There's no trace of fog in her eyes, as though the Mom I left behind in her bed was only a stranger I imagined. "All our paintings and all our stories," she says, "and now you're in the realm where they come from. How amazing is this?"

"I know! It's hard to believe, right?"

"But tell me again why you're here?"

"We're here to help Sae and Erlang end a prophecy where there's supposed to be a huge flood that destroys Zhen." The words race out of my mouth so fast that I can barely breathe (but in a good way). I can't help it. I have so much to tell. Always it's Mom who tells me the stories, but now I can finally tell her one. "We can't let Chaos win. I'm going to stop him."

Mom smiles. Somehow it makes me miss her like she's actually still back home. "Chaos, is it?"

"Yes, Chaos the demon! Let me wake up Marilla. And you have to meet Sae and Erlang and—"

"Let's let them sleep for just a bit longer. I'm actually here to tell you a myth, Astrid. A new one." Mom pats the ground beside her, so I shift closer. I feel little again, standing in front of the paintings, my fingers touching glass over silk as Mom stands beside me and spins magic with words.

"A new story?" I glance over at my sister's sleeping cat form. She's angry with me, but she'd want to know Mom's here. "But Marilla—"

"I can tell her the story later. Now, will you listen? You'll like this one."

I go quiet, too happy to argue (and Marilla might not even care to hear a new myth, anyway). I'm surprised Mom's holding *A Handbook of Ancient Chinese Myths*—how did she know I had it?

"Of course, you know the myth of Pangu," she starts, "where the universe is created out of chaos, but only with order does it finish coming true. It's famous because there's a hero—order—and there's a villain—chaos—and people love to cheer for the first as much as they love to hate the second. But there's another myth of creation, Astrid, even though it's not as popular. And it's a story about the *real* nature of chaos and order."

"Pangu's myth is a lie?" I look at her, wondering why she's never told us this before.

"Hush." She opens the book. "Just listen."

Hundun, the One Simple Shape God

A long time ago, while the world's lands and seas were still settling, there was a god with more than one name. One of his names was Hundun, and for now, that is the one I will use.

Hundun was a unique god, for he was just one simple shape. A boxy stone, if you will. He was the ruler of the Middle Sea, which separated the North and South Seas. The god of the North Sea was Shu and the god of the South was Hu, and both gods often held meetings in between. Hundun was very generous and never minded making room for the two other gods.

One day, to show how grateful they were to Hundun, Shu and Hu decided that Hundun should have seven holes in his body just as they did. The holes would be gifts, they said, since having eyes, a nose, a mouth, and ears would give Hundun the ability to finally see, smell, taste, and hear.

On the first day, they carved his mouth, and Hundun took his first breath. He was very excited to finally be able to talk, but Shu and Hu ordered him to wait.

On the second and third days they carved his nostrils, and Hundun longed to describe smell for the first time. But Shu and Hu ordered him to wait.

On the fourth and fifth days they gave him his ears, and Hundun asked to share what he could hear, but Shu and Hu ordered him to wait.

On the sixth day they carved his left eye, and Hundun begged to describe what he could see. But again, Shu and Hu ordered him to wait.

And then on the seventh day, Shu and Hu cut one last hole, giving Hundun his right eye. Finally the god of the Middle Sea was as lucky as they were! Shu and Hu then ordered Hundun to tell them everything now that he could talk, smell, hear, and see.

But instead of saying anything at all, Hundun died.

"What!" I sat up straight. "That's so unfair. Poor god."

"Have you guessed Hundun's other name yet?" Mom gives me a squeeze. "It was *Chaos*. Shu and Hu also shared another name, and it was *Order*. And in forcing Chaos into being something against his nature, Order wrongfully *killed* Chaos. So, now that you've heard his story, do you still mean to help destroy the *true* hero?"

I stare at Mom like she's a stranger. How can she think this Hundun rock is actually Chaos the demon? Or that Chaos is a hero and worthy of a silk-thread painting? "Chaos isn't the good guy, Mom. He wants to destroy all of Zhen!"

She smiles again. "He's only misunderstood. And none of it is his fault—it's yin and yang, and because order exists, so must he. Instead of helping stop the prophecy, you and Marilla should go back home."

A cloud slides over the sky and for an instant, everything goes dark. When the cloud clears away, Mom's holding a plate of my family-famous fruit dumplings.

Which is . . . weird. And her shirt—it's not pale gray elephants anymore but dark gray snakes.

Fear prickles across the back of my neck.

"You're not Mom," I whisper. "This is a dream."

"Of *course* it's me. I traveled across realms just to see you! And I even brought some of your baked dumplings for us to share." Mom's still smiling, but now her teeth—the way they shine in the moonlight—look a lot more like fangs.

"Did you know the inside of a dumpling is a symbol of harmony?" She holds out a dumpling. "The perfect balance of all different ingredients, swirling together. And yet this harmony is also imprisoned, stuck inside with no room to move."

Harmony. Balance. I think of how Grandma was always so careful picking out just the right ingredients for her meat dumplings (and how she helped me make my apple ones better). "The flavors must dance together perfectly, Astrid," she'd say, "or the taste will be uneven. Out of balance."

Mom cracks open the baked shell of a dumpling, and sugary fruit spills out all over the plate. "Only when its cage gets broken can harmony be freed. Don't you want harmony?"

I pinch the inside of my arm. *Wake up!* I want to get away from this Dream-Mom who keeps talking about dumplings. This smiley Mom who is even scarier than a Mom who looks at you without seeing you.

"You want to know something else?" Dream-Mom asks. "Harmony and chaos actually mean the same thing. Isn't that funny?"

"No, they don't. They're totally different."

"They are the same. Both mean combining things, the mixing of them. It's just that one is a hero's word and the other a villain's. And now that you know the real story of Chaos, you must let him be free."

Another cloud comes and goes; Dream-Mom and

dream-dumplings are finally gone. And a monster is in their place.

No—a *serpent*. Just like the dark gray snakes that were on Dream-Mom's shirt, except alive and a hundred times bigger (maybe even more).

Its body is all coiled up on the ground in front of me. I don't want to think about how long it really is. Twenty feet? Fifty feet? And instead of the matching giant snake head that you'd expect, the serpent's is humanlike and made out of copper. It's got a head of wild red hair, too, spiking out all over the way flames do. Eyes glowing like hot coals, orange and black all at once.

A forked tongue waggles in the dark cave of its mouth. "We need to come to an understanding, Astrid Xu. You know now how Chaos has been wronged from the beginning of time. Go home instead of helping Order imprison him again."

I try to make a noise to wake up the others but can only make a whimpering sound.

"Scream as loud as you want," the serpent hisses. "No one here will wake up. *I* am controlling this dream." It slithers toward Marilla and hisses so her fur ripples. Deep in her own dreams, my sister shudders. "But I can make their sleep very uncomfortable, if I must."

"Who are you?"

"A servant to this realm who wants nothing more than to see Chaos regain his rightful place."

I shake my head. "If Chaos *was* Hundun once, then sure, he got a bad deal. But that still doesn't mean he should flood Zhen."

The serpent slithers close, fast as lightning streaking across the ground. I back away until I hit my tree.

"How about a deal, Astrid Xu, breaker of the seal of the Scroll of Chaos? An immortal peach from the Queen Mother of the West's garden, just as you want. In exchange, you and Marilla go home. You get to save your mother, and Chaos will get his prophecy. Here—catch."

The serpent opens up its mouth wide and something tumbles out into my hand.

An immortal peach.

The shape of the peach is different from how they are in Mom's paintings. More doughnut shaped than round, and smaller than I expected—I guess I'm too used to the ones in the grocery store. The outer fuzz is super soft against my skin, something like velvet and silk and dragon's beard candy all at once. I lift the peach to my nose and right away I can tell none at home could ever be as sweet.

A peach, right here in my hand. Mom can be all better,

and everyone at home won't be in danger anymore. I've never wanted anything so badly.

But the price—it's *huge*. Can I really just give up on Sae and Erlang and Howl? On all the gods and goddesses of the myths I grew up listening to? The entire realm would be washed away because of *me*. Just like it was me who brought Chaos to life in the first place.

Me, the only person who can now stop him.

My hand trembles around the peach that suddenly feels wrong—that feels more like poison than medicine—and my confusion falls away.

"My answer is no." I glare at the serpent.

"Surely you want your mom to stop being sick? The fog of her depression gone for good? For you all to be a *real* family again?"

"Still a nope." *Uuugh*, to think that I nearly fell for this trick! That I almost trusted a serpent so I didn't have to worry about messing up again. Sae says there's nothing wrong with being scared, but it shouldn't mean forgetting to be angry. No way can I let Chaos destroy all of Zhen.

"You won't be able to stop the prophecy!" The serpent hisses and spits. "It's a waste of time to try!"

All we can do is try, anyway, I think. I smirk at the serpent, just as Erlang would. "Chaos must not be so sure if he needs you to help him make a deal."

Just like that, the peach disappears from my hand. There's a sting of regret, hot and bitter, before it fades with a flash.

The serpent uncoils, faster and faster, a wild blur in the shadows. "You've just made a terrible mistake, Astrid Xu. Your path west will be full of pain." Only its glowing coal eyes show, hot and furious. "Now, wake up—if you dare!"

FOURTEEN

"Aaaaah!"

I sit up straight, heart thumping hard in my chest.

The serpent's gone. It's just Sae, Erlang, Marilla, Howl, and me. On the ground in front of me is *A Handbook of Ancient Chinese Myths.*

It's no longer night, the sky a plum purple around the stars. I glance around; while we all slept, grim magic crept close. The woods around the small clearing are more chalky white than the emerald green they were. Moss spreads out all around like a huge snowy blanket, when just hours ago its blue reminded me of the sea. Even the air feels colder than it should, as though Chaos just swept through.

I stare at my hand, still feeling the weight of the peach. Then I remember that awful serpent and try to shake myself free of the dream. Chaos doesn't know about my plan to steal the peach, but I'll feel a million times better once it's done.

"Astrid." Sae's awake and watching me. "Are you all right?"

I guess they heard me scream. Or maybe they suspect

from my face, since they know about bad dreams, too. Not wanting to talk about it, I busy myself by sliding the handbook into the outer pocket of my backpack. "Yep, just hungry, I think."

"Ah. Growing breakfast in a minute."

By the time I use my inhaler and chew on a teeth-cleaning sprig, everyone's awake and Sae's calling us over to eat. Marilla ignores me, so I ignore her back. I was right about the argument being the worst one we've ever had.

Once all the leftovers are packed up, we leave the clearing. The trees thin away until we're in a dusty open field, big enough that I can barely see the trees on the other side. Marilla starts telling Erlang all about *Enter the Dragon* (Mom and Dad's favorite Bruce Lee movie; Marilla's only allowed to watch bits and pieces of it) while I count all the patches of brown I still see along the way.

Sae comes to a stop. "Listen—something's coming."

Erlang pushes up his helmet. His third eye looks across the field as Howl crouches, growling. "Let me try. My eye is weakened, but whatever it is might be close enough."

I listen, but all I hear is what I heard last night. "It's just the Red River, isn't it?"

"Not the river." Sae bends down and puts their hand flat on the dusty ground. "Try this."

I put my hand down. The ground is vibrating.

"An earthquake?" Marilla asks, all four of her paws pressed to the earth. "Like we get back home?"

"Not that, either." Fear fills Sae's eyes. "It's something moving. Something big."

"Nian!" Erlang shouts, slamming his helmet back down. "Running this way!"

Nian.

Ice prickles me all over as I think of the ancient village-eating monsters. Chaos must be trying to rewrite their myth next, just like he tried to rewrite Hou Yi's. I get even colder as I remember the serpent from my dream, telling me I would be sorry if I didn't go home. What if the nian are here because of me? And Chaos sent them because he's figured out who we are?

"*Real* nian?" Marilla looks up at me, forgetting to be mad. Her tail's all puffed out from fear. Her cat face says she's remembering the myth, and how the nian especially liked eating children.

"We'll hide in the trees," I tell her.

"There's no point." Sae sifts through the flowers and herbs inside their basket. "They must be Chaos's latest obstacle, and we can't hide from them forever. No, to get any farther, we'll have to face them."

I nearly tell Sae that the nian might be my fault, but I

stop. It won't make a difference now, anyway. "We need red things," I say in a rush. "Red things scare them. And things that make loud noises."

"Lion masks will scare them away, too," Marilla adds.

Sae holds out their hand. In their palm is a bunch of seeds and small plants. As they pass some to me, the seeds and plants change.

An orange flower becomes a flowy red cloak.

A blue petal turns into a paper lion mask, with a painted-gold mane and a mouth that's open mid-roar.

Finally, Sae hands me a tuft of red-and-black-striped grass—yao grass. Wondering what will come out of my clarinet this time, I stuff the yao grass into my mouth and take the instrument out of my case.

"My magic is weaker now," Sae reminds me. The ground vibrates harder. "The yao grass might change back before you want it to, so I'll tell you when to start playing."

"Okay." I quickly wrap the red cloak around myself and slip on my mask. (This might be the closest I get to being at one of those costumed balls.)

Erlang eats a tuft of yao grass and his triple-pointed spear transmutes into a long sword. The length of the blade glows; as he swings it to test, fire flows from it in an arc. "I can't complain."

Sae's straw basket becomes a mass of straw-colored

rope. "It's woven from the flesh of the gow-sweeah tree," they explain as they loop it over their shoulder, "which is known for its tenacious stickiness. Even Erlang's spear would be entrapped before it could pierce free."

Howl barks. Sae transforms a small nut from their basket into a loop of cymbals. They slip it over the dog's neck, and the cymbals smash together as Howl moves. *Clang, clang, clang!*

"Can I do something, too?" Marilla asks. "I want to help." She kicks out a back leg. "Kiyaaah!"

Erlang shakes his head. "Still such a strange sight."

Sae transforms another nut and tugs a miniature lion mask over Marilla's face. "An extra magical mask," they say. "Now you can roar like never before."

"What do you mean?" Marilla asks.

"You'll see."

"Into my cape for now," Erlang says. "If things go wrong and the nian stampede, you *are* mortal, no matter how brave you're being."

She leaps up onto Erlang's shoulder. "I'll be as loud as I can to scare them away!" she yells over the rising noise. It's the thunderous sound of hundreds of hooves hitting the ground.

I squint across the field, and through the eye holes of my mask, I see clouds of dirt racing toward us. A second later the clouds part like curtains and reveal the charging nian.

The monsters have the bodies of powerful bulls, shaggy with turquoise-blue coats. Dragon-like heads are perched on top of long necks, and they're covered in gleaming scales of the same turquoise blue. Big yellow horns spiral out of their foreheads, and their ears lie along the sides of their heads like fins on the sides of sharks. Bright orange manes flow around their thick necks, and their violet-colored eyes are like those of snakes. Rows of sharp white fangs glint and wink beneath the sun.

My stomach rolls over as the nian get closer and closer, as the first of their shrieks reach me. The sound is like jagged glass, sharper than the thunder of their stomping feet.

We have maybe a minute before they charge into us.

"Yeaahhh!" Erlang runs out into the field, red cape flying in the wind as he rushes toward the nian. The tips of Marilla's ears poke out from the folds at the top of his cape. His sword glows as he swings it through the air, moving so fast I can barely see it—only the trail of fire the sword leaves behind proves it moved at all.

Howl takes off after them, the cymbals around his neck loud and clanging. He dives into the mass of bull-like bodies and soon disappears from sight.

Some of the nian jerk back from the noise, confused. The flash of fire cuts through the fresh clouds of dust rising up from the nian's scrabbling feet. A huge roar ripples across the air (where did *that* come from?) and the nian scream in fear.

"It's working!" I turn to see if Sae's noticed. "They're getting scared—"

The immortal rushes past me. Their rope is still neatly coiled around their shoulder. But instead of diving straight into the nian the way Erlang did, Sae veers away, keeping to the outside.

"Where are you going?" I shout through the mouth hole of my lion mask. Shock's dried up all the spit in my mouth as I realize I'm about to face hundreds of charging nian all on my own.

"You'll be fine, Astrid," Sae calls back over their shoulder. "Now—start playing your clarinet!"

More dust rises and Sae disappears from view.

"Okay, you can do this," I whisper as I bring my clarinet to my mouth. *Just like with the firebirds, but keep it going until the end this time.* I take a breath, face the charging nian, and start playing.

Up ahead, more nian rear back from Erlang's flaming sword and Marilla's lion mask. Howl runs back and forth, cymbals crashing together. As nian stumble around in fear, ones in the back push past them and circle back, trapping Erlang, Marilla, and Howl inside. Dust swarms into a thick, high wall.

Panic pushes at me as I lose sight of Marilla, but I make myself keep playing, waiting for something to happen with my clarinet. Music mixes with the sounds of thunder and shrieking.

Something emerges from the end of my clarinet. But instead of silver looking like mirrors, the images floating up into the air are tiny bunches of flowers. Golden and glowing and wheat-like, they find the wind and drift up high.

A second later, color and light burst across the sky. Noises crack open the air—*boom* and *snap* and *bang.*

Firecrackers!

The nian go wild, crashing against one another as they search for escape. Another of those lionlike roars makes the air shake, and I remember Marilla's lion mask— she's the one doing all the roaring!

My heart pounds with nerves and I keep playing. *Don't push too fast. The air's getting dusty, which is bad for your asthma, so be extra careful. Breathe. And whatever you do, don't panic.*

More gold flowers drift upward. More color and light explode overhead. Noise crackles and booms and echoes its way across the trees.

The nian smash their horns together as they flail around, so confused about which way to go to get away that they don't go anywhere. I see the glow of Erlang's sword again, lines of fire drawn through the air as he swings. There's the ringing of Howl's cymbals as he darts in between the nian. Another roar from Marilla-the-lion.

One nian stumbles free from the group. It spins, uncertain, and races toward me.

I grab a breath for the next note. When I play this time, only music comes out. No sign of golden flowers.

Air gets stuck in my throat. I push through it for the next note—harder than I know I should—and a familiar tightness starts creeping back into my chest. Still no flowers.

Everything inside me seems to collapse. It's the yao grass—it must be all used up! My lion mask slips off and floats away, dissolving as it goes. My red cloak disappears from around my body. The ground shudders as the lone nian gets closer.

Keep playing! I yell at myself. *You made the air shimmer all on your own when you played for the guards! What if doing that is just another form of power?*

My fingers on the keys tremble, but just once. I ignore the growing pinched feeling and dive into the solo part of the song.

The air around my clarinet puckers and rolls, exactly as it did when we were below the Moving Sands. I keep playing, trying not to think about anything but each note as it comes. The air in front of me billows and stretches, my own kind of windstorm.

Right in front of me, the nian slows, then staggers to a stop. Its giant mane blows straight back with the force of the wind from my clarinet. Violet eyes furious, it flares its giant nostrils as it tries to push forward. But the wind just blows it back, again and again. The nian slowly tilts its head at me as the furious look in its eyes turns into one that's more like curiosity. A second later, the nian turns around and starts running again. As it charges toward the rest of the nian, the others turn to run with it. They all race off into the distance, whorls of blue and orange through swirls of dust.

I let the clarinet drop from my mouth. "Wow," I breathe. A tuft of orange fur untangles from my hair and I grab it midair. I tuck it into the front pocket of my jeans. Another souvenir.

Marilla runs over. She stares at me, almost as though I'm a stranger. "You stopped that nian with just music. All by yourself, no yao grass. How did you do that?"

"I don't know. I just played and the air changed. It became this wind that pushed the nian away." I glance down at the clarinet in my hand. "I guess this really is a form of power here."

"Sae and Erlang have been telling you that this whole time."

I nod, grinning.

"Did you hear me roar?" Marilla asks, grinning back.

"Yes! You really helped, cat or not."

Her grin slides away. "I'm still mad at you, by the way. About what you said about me not caring about Mom as much as you. But I'm also glad you didn't become nian food." She moves away before I can say anything.

"Thanks," I mutter under by breath. "And, fine, I'm still mad, too." But it's a lie—I'm not that mad anymore. (And I'm sorry about what I said, too.) I guess I just wish she understood why I have to steal a peach. Or maybe I just wish that I never told her in the first place. Maybe then we wouldn't be having this argument that's already lasting too long. What happens when an argument stays so big that the being mad part also can't ever disappear? What if it just stays like this between us until it's too late to fix it?

Erlang and Howl emerge from the still-swirling dirt. The warrior slides his spear back into its holder and nods at me, appearing pleased. "Astrid, you played the music of firecrackers. Just what the nian hate most."

"They really did hate it, didn't they?" I say. "I didn't understand the flowers, though."

"Those were flowers of the bamboo plant."

"Oh, from their myth!" I remember now. How it was dried bamboo that the visitor set on fire for noise.

"Where's Sae?" Erlang asks, trying to see through the dust. His hand goes to his helmet to use his third eye.

"Over here," Sae's voice calls out. As the last of the dirt falls back to the ground, we turn to see them standing off to the side.

Lying at their feet are two thrashing nian. They're trapped in straw-colored nets—I was wrong about Sae changing their basket only into rope.

I automatically leap back. The memory of the nian charging toward me is still way too fresh.

The monsters glare at us through the nets, their violet eyes cold and watchful. Their turquoise-blue scales shine and gleam just as coldly. They open their mouths and shriek at us, their fangs as sharp as knives. There's also a stink to them I didn't notice before. It's even worse than Bear after he gets caught in the rain.

If they've been trying to fight their way out, they've already stopped. The gow-sweeah material of the nets is as sticky as Sae promised, so the arms and legs of the nian are tangled up and stuck together, and the nets are stuck to the ground so the beasts can't move an inch.

"I can't believe you caught them," Marilla says, sounding too awed to be scared. Beside her, Howl growls at the nian.

"Stay back," Sae says softly. "The nets are about to fall apart. My magic is only barely keeping them together."

Erlang scowls at the nian and turns to Sae. "What are you doing? Let them go."

"I want them." The immortal doesn't look good. Their skin looks shiny and clammy and they have big gray smudges beneath their eyes that I'm pretty sure are new. I glance over really quickly at Erlang; his eyes have dark smudges beneath them, too.

"What do you want them for?" Erlang asks.

"Let me secure them first and then I'll tell you. The nets—it's dangerous—"

"You're right, this *is* dangerous!" Erlang keeps glaring at the nian, their huge dragon-like jaws open against the nets. "They are Chaos's work. Who knows what he might try through them?"

Sae's eyes are nearly black against their paled skin. "Will you actually listen?"

"We should already be on our way."

"I caught them *because* they are the demon's work. If we can get them back to Chaos in a way that makes him believe we've been defeated, it might buy us some time. If he thinks he's already won, he might just savor his new reign over Zhen before destroying it for good."

"And how would you send him this message?"

Sae's mouth tightens. "I haven't thought of that quite yet."

"Perhaps we should each sacrifice a finger," Erlang says sarcastically. "We can weave them into the beasts' manes for Chaos to find and believe we've been eaten."

Erlang talking about food makes something click in my head. "Wait!" I leap up. "I've got an idea that might work. About buying us some time."

FIFTEEN

"Tell me," Sae says. "And hurry."

"I'll show you; it'll be faster." I move closer to the nets and unzip my backpack. I take out a leaf of leftover membao.

"Astrid, move back," Erlang warns. "You can't get that close."

"I'll be careful. And it'll be okay—you'll see in a second."

At the smell of the food, the nian go even more nuts. Yowling and trying to lunge toward the net.

"In the myth," I say over my shoulder while keeping one eye on the monsters, "nian left their mountain home because they were hungry. And they only ate humans once they couldn't find crops or animals." I roll up the leaf of membao and hold it out to one of the nian.

Right away it stops snarling. It works its blue-scaled snout through one of the small holes in the net and sniffs the membao. A second later, dragon-like jaws snap at the rolled-up leaf, barely missing my fingers. I feed the second nian next, and after its jaws gobble it down, neither of the nian looks at me like I'm supposed to be the meal.

Instead, they just sniff the air for more membao, their purple eyes blinking calmly at me. *More?*

I turn to the others. Everyone's looking at me with confused expressions (even Howl cocks his head).

"Don't you see?" I ask. "It's just like how Chaos made the firebirds as close as he could to the real thing. He made the nian the same way; they always want food. And if they're always wanting to eat, then they can be bribed to do what we want. As long as the membao lasts, anyway."

"You want to tame these beasts with food?" Erlang only looks more confused. "Why tame them?"

"We're going to ride them west. Like horses. Nian like to run, right? We'll get to Kunlun Mountain even faster."

Sae laughs. "Brilliant, Astrid. I wish I could have thought of it."

"Not bad, mortal, not bad at all!" Erlang roughly claps my back.

Before I can really bask in the moment, Sae collapses and falls to one knee.

Erlang crouches down, concern making him scowl. "Let go of the nets now. I have my spear as well as my bow and arrow. And Howl is here. Not to mention the food."

Marilla hops onto Erlang's shoulder and I hold my breath.

Erlang grips his spear. "Okay—now."

Sae nods, and the nets pull away from the nian and off the dirt. In midair, the nets unweave themselves back into rope and then back into Sae's straw basket. When it's all done, the basket drops to the ground.

The nian blink their purple eyes at us. *More?* One yawns.

"Phew," I say.

Erlang pulls Sae to their feet. "You should have told us from the beginning what you wanted to do."

"I know, I'm sorry." Sae's already less pale, though they still seem drained. "I don't know why I didn't. Perhaps I already sensed you wouldn't like the idea."

"Perhaps. But you've never kept an idea from me before. You know, if Chaos wanted to distract us from fighting him, one way is to keep us from working together."

I glance around as though I can spot the demon spying on us. How do you beat something that's somehow all around you yet also nowhere at once? I rub goose bumps from my arm.

Marilla must feel something, too, because the fur along her back ruffles. Like me, she might also be remembering Sae and Erlang arguing badly beneath the Moving Sands. "Bad vibes all around here," she says. "Can we leave now?"

Sae nods. "The Red River is close—we'll find it and follow its course. I'd been hoping we could travel by water, but my magic is too weak to hold on to a raft now, not to mention we'd be fighting the current the whole way. But it doesn't matter anymore because Astrid's idea of using the nian as horses is much better."

I put away my clarinet, just sliding it into my backpack whole (sorry, Mom and Dad). Inside my backpack there's also our stash of leftover membao, and I hold out the bundle of soft leaves. "How far will this take us with the nian? All the way to Kunlun Mountain?"

"Not quite," Sae says slowly. "Not just because of the amount of membao, but because the Red River doesn't actually go all the way."

"Aw." Marilla deflates.

I look from Sae to Erlang, puzzled. "Didn't you say there was nothing else?"

They exchange a glance. It's the same glance they exchanged last night when they both said only the Red River was left before reaching Kunlun. But now I know that they lied.

"The Red River eventually meets the Weak Water," Sae admits. "*That's* the last obstacle between us and the mountain. There is no getting around it, for it fully encircles Kunlun."

"The Weak Water?" I grab *A Handbook of Ancient Chinese Myths* from its pocket and find the page.

The Weak Water

Enter at your own risk, for even a weightless shadow will sink.

"Only divine beings are able to travel the Weak Water," Erlang says. "And that's only if we travel over it by cloud. Mortals aren't meant to cross at all."

I already know Marilla and I can't travel by cloud—our mortal weight keeps us tied to the earth. Otherwise, we'd already be at Kunlun. We might already be back home with Mom saved. A nervous feeling fills me as I put the book back. "Is that why you didn't want to tell us? We're stuck now unless we backtrack or something?" There's no time.

"It's not that we didn't want to tell you," Sae says. "Only that Erlang and I wanted to wait until we had some idea of how to get you and Marilla across. A way that wouldn't make you decide to go home instead."

"How bad can your idea be?" I can't imagine giving up on the idea of saving Mom. Just like I can't give up on saving Sae and Erlang and Howl, either.

Sae and Erlang exchange yet another look.

Marilla's ears flick at super speed. "Wow, it must be *really* bad if Erlang isn't bugging us about how we're just making things harder again."

Erlang's expression goes sour. "The plan is dangerous. You can't cross the Weak Water as mortals and we can't make you temporarily divine."

"Then what's the plan?" I ask. The violet eyes of the nian track us. They're probably getting hungrier by the minute.

"If we can't make you fully immortal, then we'll just have to make the mortal part of you smaller. As in, make *you* smaller."

Now it's Marilla and me who look at each other. All kinds of alarm bells are preparing to go off in my head.

"What's *that* mean?" I ask.

"We're going to shrink you," Erlang says casually. "Freed of your earthbound weight, the travel cloud will be tricked into sensing you are immortal."

Alarm bells blare. "You've got to be kidding me."

"*Shrink* us?" Marilla actually doesn't sound very scared at all. "Why didn't you just do that at the very start? We could have been traveling by cloud this entire time!"

"We can only shrink you right by the shores of the Weak Water," Sae explains. "The shrinking elixir is made from the shells of the ruby snail—in ancient times, the shells were fed to criminals to shrink away dangerous thoughts, and now we just use them to bring down swellings. And though the ruby snails are found near water in many parts of Zhen, it's the ones by the Weak Water that we want. The Weak Water dissolves the shells, and its dark magic forms the elixir. So it's right there on its shores where the elixir is strongest. That's where it needs to be ingested if we want you to stay shrunken for as long as possible."

"How small do we get to shrink?" Marilla asks excitedly.

"Small enough to go unnoticed."

"How do we *un*shrink?" I ask. What if we shrink too much? Would we just disappear completely? No wonder they didn't want to tell us this plan!

"The effect will naturally wear off," Sae says.

"Are you sure?" The familiar knot of panic twinges. "What if Chaos's grim magic has affected the elixir and we never grow back? Or we grow back at the wrong time and we're still up in the sky? What if your travel cloud falls apart too early?"

"That's why this plan is dangerous," Erlang says. "But it's also the only way for you to cross the Weak Water in order to get to Kunlun Mountain."

"Stop worrying, will you?" Marilla says, not hiding how

exasperated she is with me since she's still mad (I wonder when she'll be done). She does her Bruce Lee kick.

Be like water.

A nian roars. I go over and feed it a leaf of membao, my heart full of a roar of its own.

The call of Kunlun Mountain.

• • •

"This is the best roller coaster in all the universe!"

Marilla's perched on my shoulder as we ride, and her shout floats up above the thumping of our nian's running feet. We didn't formally give our nian a name, but in my head, it's Beans. That's the name I picked out for my future cat back when I was five, before we found out Dad's allergic. I've also decided that Beans is a girl nian, and it's almost easy to forget how she'll eat us up in a second if we let her get too hungry.

I pat her through the thick orange mane encircling her neck. The fringe of fur is where her body changes from dragon to bull, from turquoise-blue scales to turquoise-blue coat. I only have one slice of membao left, but it should keep Beans full enough to bring us all the way to the Weak Water.

Sae and Erlang are behind us on their own nian. Sae's seated in front and in charge of feeding while Erlang uses the edge of his spear to guide their nian along the water.

Howl runs on the ground alongside them, sunshine flashing off his new collar of ringing cymbals.

Beside us, the Red River flows. It really *is* red normally; Sae tells me that the river's bed and shores are made of a red-tinted mud that colors the water as it flows. But right now, it's more like pale pink lemonade being poured out of a pitcher, since so much of the mud it touches has turned ghostly white from grim magic. If I look really carefully, once in a while I'll see a batch of ruby snails along the shore, coin-sized disks the color of pink cotton candy. (When I pointed out how they were already touched by grim magic, Sae shouted back that we'd have to dig deep for untouched ones once we reached the Weak Water.)

Already the Red River's moving much faster than it was just minutes ago, its rumble closer to a shout than a whisper. It's gotten deeper and narrower, too, no longer as flat or calm, as we get closer to Kunlun Mountain. And though we still can't see the mountain itself, we *can* see its enormous divine cloud cover. I only have to glance up to imagine all the jade cliffs behind it. The golden soil and silver rocks and trees that are so full of peaches their branches dip to the ground.

"Wheee!" Marilla yells in delight, practically right into my ear.

"Will you quit bellowing so loud?" I yell back.

"Sorry, I can't help it!" Her ears and whiskers fly back with the wind. "Wheee!"

I roll my eyes, but I guess I don't really mind. Riding together on Beans *is* a lot like riding the roller coaster together. Every summer we'd go, and for just a few minutes, squashed into our seats together like this, we'd forget whatever we'd been arguing about. Marilla whoops again and I grab ahold of Beans's mane and steer her through a slight turn.

Behind us, Sae calls out, "Just fed our nian the last piece of membao!"

As though Beans understood them, she twists her long dragon's head back and screeches. I toss our final slice of membao into her jaws. I pat her neck again. *Stay full, okay?*

"It's all right," Erlang says. "We're nearly there."

I squint out into the sun, and a ribbon of darkness pops up along the horizon.

The Weak Water.

The Red River begins to curve again, and I grab ahold of Beans's mane again to steer her. But this time, she fights me. She begins to shriek. From behind, I hear the second nian start shrieking, too.

"I think they're hungry again!" I shout. Now Beans is no longer Beans but the nian who wants to swallow up whole villages. Dread swims fast and loose behind my ribs. "But we just fed them!"

"The membao must be losing its magic!" Sae shouts.

Beans struggles harder against my hold on her mane. She snaps her jaws wildly at the air and stretches her dragon head back toward us. Her yellow horn and sharp white teeth flash in the sun. Marilla squeaks in fear.

"It's just a little bit farther!" Erlang yells. Without turning around, I imagine his face, as fierce in his painting back home.

And he's right. The dark gray ribbon of the Weak Water swells and fattens as we get closer. Its shore lies in front, a near-black strip. Buried inside will be pockets of ruby elixir.

But it's still too far for us to outrun two ferocious nian.

Beans screams and snarls. As her mane blows from her wild violet eyes, I see the nian from earlier, staring at me almost curiously through the wind of my clarinet, and something tingles along my spine.

"Wait, let me try something!" I twist around and yank out my clarinet from my backpack. I'm glad now that I didn't take it apart last time so I don't have to struggle putting it together (who knew I'd be rewarded for being lazy?).

"What are you *doing*?" Marilla shouts. Her claws dig

hard into my shoulder. "Are you nuts? Where are you try-ing to make the nian go by playing? Especially with us still on them?"

"Just hold on!"

I start playing.

At first, nothing changes. Beans is still freaking out, and I can barely keep her straight by pressing my knees into her sides. Behind me, Erlang smashes the length of his spear against shining blue scales, trying to keep his and Sae's nian going. Howl barks along, sensing his own-er's growing panic.

But then the sound of my clarinet rises over the thun-der of hooves, and the nian start to slow. No longer running now but closer to trotting. Like a horse. Beans swishes her head back and forth, and I get a glimpse of her violet eyes. No longer wild but calm. Now too curious about the strange music she's hearing to be furious.

"Keep playing, Astrid," Sae says behind us. They laugh, and there's relief in their voice.

"You have two new fans," Erlang chimes in. He whistles as Howl bounds ahead for Marilla to wave to.

I keep playing, my heart rushing the way the Red River was rushing before we left it behind. In front of us, the Weak Water now fills the horizon. Up this close, there's white in the water and on the sand, looking like whitecaps on top of waves and seafoam collected on the beach. But it's nothing but Chaos's spell. Just grim magic. Beans slows to a walk, shaking out her orange mane and sniffing the air every few seconds. When her hooves touch the edge of the water, she comes to a stop.

Marilla leaps off and runs back toward the shore before she can be eaten. Still playing, I swing my legs over Beans's side and carefully slide off onto the sand. I keep as far from her teeth and horn as I can, just in case. But her violet eyes are calmer than I've ever seen them, glowing and watchful but not in a hungry way. I dare to pat her neck once more before backing off onto the sand.

Sae and Erlang climb off and step onto the shore, and Erlang taps the edge of his spear along the blue scales of their nian. The animal turns and strides off toward the Red River, back the way we came. Beans looks at me once more before swinging around and following.

I let my clarinet slip from my mouth. "Bye, Beans," I whisper. I'm sad to see her go, but I know it's for the best: It's kind of impossible to have a pet that sees you as a meal unless you serenade them 24-7. "Thanks for the ride."

Erlang tucks away his spear and walks up to me. "I'm impressed! How did you know your music would calm them like that?"

"Just a lucky hunch." Face flushed, I pat my clarinet

just as I patted Beans's neck and put it away (properly this time; I don't think I'll be riding another nian anytime soon).

"Lucky, but also smart." Sae grins, shaking sand from the hem of their blue silk robe. "You used Chaos's own magic against him, Astrid. See? You do have a power of your own here."

"Its eyes changed," I explain. "That first nian I chased away, back in the field. As I played and it watched me. Like my music was finally loud enough to cover up whatever Chaos had told it." Even if it was temporary. And just in time, too. I remember the glint of Beans's teeth and shiver.

Sae stares out along the shore. Little patches of ruby snails dot the sand, but they are as pale pink as the ones by the Red River. The immortal ignores them. "All right, everyone, time to dig. We have some shrinking to do."

SIXTEEN

Erlang whistles and Howl races over. Sae takes something from their basket and holds it out for the dog to sniff.

"These are from the ruby shrub," Sae says of the tiny dark red seeds, which have just a few specks of white on them. "Its seeds smell the same as that of the ruby snail. More so than any of the snails we can see right now, since they're already asleep."

Howl gets a good whiff and promptly takes off running. We watch as he zigzags back and forth, searching for ruby snails belowground. Marilla races up to join him. Their tracks form wild patterns in the sand (while still avoiding all the white blotches of grim magic taking over the shore).

Howl stops and barks. He paws at a spot on the black sand.

"He's found something!" Marilla calls out.

By the time we get there, Howl's already dug into the sand. Wet black clumps fly out as his gray paws disappear into a growing hole. Soon he stops digging and moves away. Erlang grins and rubs the dog's head.

Sae and I peer into the hole. Red liquid fills the

bottom. The immortal takes a cream-colored flower from their straw basket, drops it into the hole, then plucks it back out. All the creamy petals are now ruby red, soaked with the elixir. Sae tears off half a dozen petals and hands them to me.

"Each petal covers a portion of time," they say. "Enough to keep you small until after we've crossed." They tear off half a dozen more and set them on top of Marilla's paw. They go through their basket again, collecting clarity flowers to call for a cloud.

All the yellow of the blossoms are now mottled with white.

Sae gathers them into one hand. "With their magic put together, they should still work. Hopefully." They hold them up to the wind and blow.

Magic whisks away the weakened blossoms, carrying them high until they're out of sight. A minute passes and then another. Finally, a large cloud forms in the air in front of us.

Sae doesn't hide their sigh of relief. "Good. I was getting worried."

Erlang pushes in black sand to fill the hole back up. "It still made it. Let's take that as a good sign."

"You're right. Astrid, Marilla? Time for the elixir."

I hand Sae my backpack and glance down at my sister.

She's still not scared at all, and I tell myself I'm not, either. I stuff my share of petals into my mouth as she eats hers from her paw.

I'm about to ask Marilla if ruby snails taste the same to her as they do to me (which is like SweeTarts candy, one of her favorites) when I remember we're still kind of fighting. Before I can turn away, she disappears.

Or, not disappear, but—

I glance down at the ground.

A tiny dollhouse cat. Canary-yellow eyes no bigger than cake sprinkles.

I stare at this miniature version of my cat sister. One misstep from Howl and it's goodbye Marilla.

The world suddenly pulls back. Now she's the size of a regular cat again, and Sae, Erlang, and Howl are giants.

I fall on my butt. My hands land on grains of black sand as big as golf balls. When Howl comes over to sniff, he's bigger than the world. Dodging him, I feel the way I did when I first got to Zhen, full of wonder and shock. *How can this be real?*

Marilla claws a tiny bit of travel cloud free and pats it like she's making a snowball.

"Excellent," Sae says, looking at Marilla and me. They crouch and we jump onto their hand. Holding us, Sae steps onto the cloud. Erlang takes my backpack and he and Howl step on next.

For a second the cloud dips under our weight. But barely—it bounces right back up. Sae sets us down and I take a few steps. It's a lot like walking across Jasper's trampoline, except fluffier. He and Libby would kill for this (not the Weak Water–being-beneath-us part, though).

The cloud starts to lift. Higher and higher and higher.

I drop to the floor and peek over the edge. We must be twenty stories high! Down below, the Weak Water appears solid black instead of gray and the seafoam as hard as a plane of ice. Sunlight hits the water's surface, as bright as cold fire.

The cloud starts drifting west. I watch the water shimmer and dance. When I start to feel dizzy, I move away from the edge.

"We can't go any faster, unfortunately," Erlang says. Lines of concentration form between his brows as he uses his demigod power to keep the cloud moving. "Magic stretched too thin *will* snap."

Sae nods. The gray smudges beneath their eyes are even darker. "We'll get there soon."

Howl curls up in a ball and seems to go to sleep (I guess cloud travel must be pretty boring for him by now).

Marilla claws more bits of cloud free and starts piling it on top of him.

I go back to peering over the edge. The view hasn't changed, so I look in the direction of Kunlun Mountain. It doesn't seem much closer, either. But from this height, the divine cloud is a lot more interesting looking, its outer layers swirling and shifting and spinning. Sun filters through it and shadows dance from inside the layers like gray whirls of smoke. One of the whirls moves snake-like and the memory of my nightmare comes crashing back. The hissing serpent. The Dream-Mom.

I move closer to the others. "It was my fault the nian charged this morning," I blurt out.

Everyone stares. Even Howl wakes up to stare.

"What are you talking about?" Erlang says.

"I had a nightmare. There was a serpent who said it served the realm, and it said if Marilla and I didn't go home, we'd all be punished." I swallow as the feeling of the dream comes back. The sweet smell of the peach, the serpent growing as it uncoiled. "If I listened, then maybe the nian wouldn't have come."

"It was just a bad dream," Sae reassures me. "And fears have a way of surfacing when we're asleep, that's all. It wasn't real."

"It sure felt real." As real as having to pick up the

handbook from the ground after I woke up, even though it was in my backpack when I fell asleep.

"Think about it," Erlang says. "If the serpent served the realm as it said, then why wouldn't it want you to stop the flood? Dreams are just more of those mind games you and Marilla spoke of."

"It said there was another myth about chaos and order that we don't know about," I explain. "Not just Pangu's version."

Sae frowns. "Which myth?"

"The myth of Hundun."

"'Hundun.'" Sae repeats the name and keeps frowning.

I nod. "The serpent said that Hundun stood for chaos, but instead of chaos being a bad thing, chaos is actually just another way of saying harmony. Like how you can describe the inside of a dumpling as messy chaos *or* a balance of flavors. So, two gods who represent order come along and meet Hundun. But instead of just balancing out chaos the way order does in Pangu's myth, in Hundun's story, order *kills* chaos by forcing it into something it can't be. And that's why the serpent says it's only right to leave Chaos alone. Because he's actually Hundun reborn, and it's order that is actually evil."

Marilla sniffs. "*Order* is the bad guy? *We're* the villains? No way."

"Astrid, did this serpent have a copper human face?" Erlang asks slowly. "And wild red hair?"

"How did you—" Something like a cold finger touches my spine. "That serpent is real, isn't it?"

"Yes. It was Chaos the demon."

I'm so shocked, it takes a few seconds for my brain to react. "I thought Chaos's form wasn't done yet. How do you know he's a serpent?"

"His form might *not* be done," Sae says. "That might be why he could only appear to you in a dream to try to stop you, instead of while you were awake. But we know it's him because Chaos is not actually new to Zhen. He existed long ago and was a serpent back then, too. He's merely been reborn now."

Erlang glowers. "It was our mistake for assuming the demon in the Scroll of Chaos was a new one instead of old. In calling himself by the new name of Chaos, we were all fooled."

"Yes, there's a reason why he chose to tell you the myth of Hundun, Astrid," Sae says. "It shows the nature of chaos in the best light in comparison to that of order. But there are many different myths about chaos, each true in its own way. And now you need to hear the myth about Chaos's ancestor. It'll explain why Chaos wants to flood Zhen."

"I already know about his ancestor," I say. "That's Hundun."

"Chaos *is* reborn from Hundun, but he's also reborn from another. And that is Gonggong, the ancient water god."

Sae takes *A Handbook of Ancient Chinese Myths* from the pocket of my backpack and begins to read:

Gonggong Who Tried to Destroy the World

Many years ago, long before the world had settled into what we know today and everything that is ancient now was still new, there was a god named Gonggong. He was the god of water whose heart was greedy and cruel. He not only desired power but he also quite enjoyed seeing things destroyed (which he could not help, as his qi was always in poor balance, and so all that was good inside him was always overshadowed by that which was bad).

Being the water god of his time, Gonggong was in charge of the world's rivers. This meant he had to descend to the mortal realm and chart all the rivers' courses. He also had to watch their levels to keep them from flooding and destroying all the world's towns and villages. It must be said that he only really liked his job whenever he secretly allowed a river to flood. For it was in his nature to like all the chaos as water overcame dwellings and people ran for their lives.

Soon, as a powerful god of the Heavens, Gonggong decided he deserved more power. When a new Supreme Ruler was to be chosen, Gonggong tried to claim it—to reign over the world would suit him perfectly. More than that, as Supreme Ruler, he would be able to create as much chaos as he wanted.

But he was challenged for the duty by Zhurong, the god of fire, who also lived in the Heavens. While Zhurong didn't have a fighting serpent's body, he required *two* dragons to travel by, for the weight of his power was too great to be carried by one. Gonggong had met his match—for while the water god's nature burned for chaos, Zhurong's short temper burned just as hot.

The Heavens had never seen such a fight. Gonggong uncoiled his great serpent's body to try to knock the fire god from the sky while Zhurong commanded his dragons to aim their fire at the water god. The gods fought hard for days. Eventually, it was Zhurong who dealt the winning blow, and Gonggong fell to the earth.

The water god landed at the base of sacred Mount Buzhou, one of the sky pillars on Earth that held up the Heavens. For many moments, Gonggong lay on the ground, unable to bear his defeat. Humiliation turned into fury and the need for revenge filled his heart. If he could not rule the world, then the world would end in chaos.

Gonggong drew himself upright. He let the power build up

once more in his great serpent's body. Using all his strength, he unleashed himself at Mount Buzhou.

Thunder split the air as the sacred mountain broke. One half of the earth lifted toward the Heavens while the other half sank low. As the sky pillar crashed downward, a part of the sky came down with it. The ground burst open with the impact and the earth's many rivers began flooding forth, drowning whole towns and villages.

Gonggong ran and hid from the chaos he set forth, feeling victorious after all.

But the water god was wrong. He had not ended the world. The goddess Nüwa, the Great Mother of humans, appeared to repair all the damage. She collected different colored stones—

"Oh, I know this part!" Marilla says excitedly.

I look at her, an odd sting in my throat. I can't believe how *non*-excited she is about myths when we're home. I guess it's at home where they remind her of stuff that hurts, though. Not high up in the sky in a realm of magic.

Sae puts the book away and smiles at my sister. "Go on."

"Well, we never heard the version that included Gonggong breaking the world. We always just heard the part about Nüwa patching up the sky with different colored stones, and the different colors are why we see colors in the clouds. She stuffs forests into all the cracks in the ground to stop the flooding. Then she sacrifices a giant tortoise and uses its four legs to prop up the sky again. And that's how Nüwa saves the world."

"What happened to Gonggong afterward?" I ask Sae.

"He was forever banished from the Heavens and spent the rest of his life in exile. But now he's back as Chaos, and by flooding the realm, he'll finally beat order."

"He will strike at Mount Buzhou," Erlang declares. "The prophecy never said where the flood would start, but now that we know it's Gonggong, we just have to get to the weapon on Kunlun Mountain before he grows strong enough to break the sky pillar."

A cold draft brushes along my arm. I glance down and my heart pounds.

There's a crack in the cloud. It's wide enough for me to see the Weak Water through it, a wedge of black reflecting the sun. Sae and Erlang's magic is growing weaker.

"Hey," I croak out, my throat gone dry. "The travel cloud. It's—"

An instant later, a *second* hole opens up. This one's right in the middle of the cloud. It's big enough for someone to fall through (even Erlang, the tallest of us). The cloud shakes and drops, and my stomach drops with it, like we're in an elevator that's about to crash.

"Aaah!" Marilla tries to paw bits of cloud over to cover the hole. "What do we do?"

"Erlang!" Sae's voice is frantic. Their eyes go back and forth between the cracks. "Can you try closing them?"

As they say this, a third crack opens up right in front of where they're seated. It's even bigger than the last one. Sae freezes and goes pale as they stare down at the Weak Water below. Their old fear glows off them like a fever until even Howl is whimpering.

It'll be okay, Sae! I want to shout. But the cloud is still shaking and I'm not sure at all.

Erlang swears loudly in Chinese. His eyes are narrowed with worry as he glares out at the sky. "I can't, not without risking even more opening up! We're also keeping the cloud moving, Sae, don't forget. Our magic can only go so thin!"

The cloud wobbles and keeps dropping. The world swings and sways, like a cradle being pushed too high, and Erlang swears again. Marilla utters a half scream and her claws dig into the cloud, trying to hold on. My stomach rolling, I look down into the crack beside me. A tiny bit of brown land now lies above the black water.

"I see the opposite shore!" I shout. "We just need the cloud to hold together for a little bit longer!"

Howl starts barking and I glance over.

Marilla's staring at her paws, which are back to their regular size. It looks funny, like she's wearing oversized mitts, and my stomach drops even more. "Nooooo!" she wails, her eyes wide yellow orbs as the rest of her finishes growing back.

Sae and Erlang lower to a crouch to keep from falling over. Marilla leaps onto Erlang's back and crawls into a fold of his cape.

I stare at my own tiny hands. I watch as they stretch back to my regular human-sized ones. Then it's my legs and feet, growing like weeds. It feels, weirdly enough, like being tickled all over. I'm Astrid Xu, typical human kid once more, short but not *that* short. And definitely back to earthbound weight.

This is bad, I think as the cloud starts to dive and skate across the sky, out of control. Really *bad*.

My backpack rolls into me with a giant smack. I stare at it, thinking fast, and start fumbling for the zipper. I take out my clarinet and put it together with cold and clumsy fingers.

"The yao grass," Sae says, watching me and shaking their head. "I don't know how strong it is anymore!"

"It's okay, I won't need it." If I can make a nian think it's a horse, then maybe I can bring us to shore, too. I think of the air around my clarinet shimmering, ruffling and twisting, but this time instead of the air being around my clarinet, it's going to wrap around the travel cloud to keep it all together. And instead of protecting me from a charging nian, it's going to keep us from falling over into the Weak Water. *Don't think about what'll happen if you mess up. Just think about what you need to do.*

The cloud begins to steady as soon as I start playing.

"It's working!" Marilla says from inside the folds of Erlang's cape.

"Keep playing!" Erlang says. "Sae and I will keep the cloud moving."

I nod, not stopping. I dare to peek through one of the cracks in the cloud—there's even more brown shore showing now. *Almost there!*

A long shadow falls over us—something's crossing the sun. Thinking that it's just a regular cloud, I don't look to check.

But then the shadow *slithers*. Exactly as a serpent would.

My clarinet slips from my mouth as a gray whirl of smoke slides across the sky. It's the same one I saw earlier, moving just enough like a snake that it reminded me of my dream.

Chaos.

The demon is bigger now, longer and more solid so that it's actually close to being snake shaped. Sae's right about him not being all the way formed yet, but it won't be long.

The long whirl of smoke swooshes closer to us. As the demon passes by, the travel cloud wobbles hard. A dull roar comes and goes.

Sae's eyes are on the smoky snake as baby Chaos prepares to come again to try to spill us off. The immortal's fear of falling into the water shows all across their face. Watching them brings me back to the night of Winter Fest, how I also wanted to run from the stage but couldn't.

"Astrid, start playing again!" Sae shouts.

I do, but I'm shaken now. All I see in my head is a huge serpent's body, a copper human face, and wild red hair. My notes come out uneven, all broken up. Without power.

The whirl of smoke heads straight for us. The dull roar sharpens.

Keep it together, you're so close!

I gather up air and push the high notes from my lungs. They ring out, steady and true and even more loudly than the sound of roaring. The travel cloud steadies.

Baby Chaos comes to a stop right before he reaches us. The wind from my clarinet pushes at him, and the edges of his smoky form begin to fray and tatter. Baby Chaos slithers left and right, trying to get closer, but can't. A second later the remains of the long gray whirl flick away angrily, off to steal more qi so it can re-form and finally finish taking shape. Become the most powerful of all.

Down below, the world's nearly all brown shore—we've almost finished crossing the Weak Water.

Before I can play any more of the song, the hugest tremor yet violently shakes the cloud.

"Hold on!" Erlang bellows.

But both my hands are on my clarinet. I flip over the side of the cloud and free-fall through the air.

"Astriiiiid!" Marilla yells.

I just have time to realize that I've never heard her sound so scared and then I crash into the Weak Water.

SEVENTEEN

Icy water races over me and swallows up the world. There's nothing but darkness, cold and stinging against my eyes. Panic blares like a train horn going at full blast. Hugging my clarinet to my chest as if it can help me breathe, I start trying to kick my way back to the surface.

But it's the Weak Water. Where nothing floats and everything sinks (even a weightless shadow). I keep kicking, but I might as well be kicking at air, and my dive stays endless. My chest aches like never before and breathing becomes a sort of dream, as hazy and wild as the thoughts rushing through my head.

Did Sae and Erlang manage to get the travel cloud to shore? If Marilla's okay, does she think I'm dead? Might she even be sad? Why was I so stubborn to keep fighting with her, anyway, when we both want just the same thing in the end?

Marilla, I'm so sorry, I never meant to leave you here on your own. Help Sae and Erlang and Howl save Zhen, okay? I know I was supposed to be the one, but if we've always been better together, that means you're just as good as me. I know it.

Mom, is your fog like this darkness, all around you with not even a hint of light? No air, keeping you from breathing, from being? I wish both of us could escape. I wish so much—

Dad, don't forget to—

Sae, about the—

Erlang Howl—

Libby Jasper Bear—

Spring Revival! and my solo. I'm not supposed to be scared anymore, but I still am I'm so scared right now—

I keep falling, faster and faster. Still in my dive, my entire body screaming for air, I black out.

EIGHTEEN

I wake up coughing and spitting out water. When I'm done, I stand up and look around, squeezing water out of my sweater. *How am I still alive? Where is everyone else?*

I'm in the middle of some kind of street. I assumed the Weak Water was bottomless, but instead it seems there's a city beneath. The street's made up of earthy-orange terra-cotta bricks (I recognize the material from Dad's gardening containers), and houses sit behind front ledges that double as fences. All of this is terra-cotta, too.

I glance up. The sky's dark purple, and there are waves, just like the ocean—I'm looking at the Weak Water from below. When this part of Zhen's magic finally loses all its qi, the Weak Water will come storming down. So far, though, there aren't any signs of grim magic down here. Just how deep into the earth am I?

Remembering that I fell with my clarinet, I start searching for it, frantic. It would have sunk with me—it has to be close!

I find it farther down along the street—it must have rolled after landing. When I pick it up, my heart sinks at what I see. The ligature—the silver piece that holds the reed and mouthpiece together—is half twisted off. If I lose the rest of it, the reed will probably get lost, too. Not only that, the bottom bell piece has a crack running through it—my notes won't sound right anymore.

Great. I wipe the instrument off on my shirt as best as I can (my shirt's not exactly clean) and start walking. I need to get out of here and find the others. They must have made it to shore; otherwise they'd be here, too, after being dumped off the cloud just as I was.

It doesn't take long to decide the whole place is deserted. I walk street after street, but see no one. The only sound is my own breathing, shallow and anxious.

"Hello?" I call out once. But no one answers. The terra-cotta streets seem never-ending and soon I find myself in an alley. Here the ground is rich soil around round stones; thick draping greenery hangs over wood fences. I've lost sense of where I've turned. Am I only getting farther from the others? From Kunlun Mountain?

I start to run, trying to smooth out the fear starting to build inside my chest. The alley turns. Now there are stands of dense shrubs and bushes. Thick-branched trees covered with vines. Ground cover of moss and grasses studded with tiny fuzzy flowers.

When I hear a voice coming from somewhere up ahead, I skid to a stop. I tiptoe to the next turn in the alley and peek my head around.

It's a person (I think? Zhen has all kinds of creatures), crouched over some purple blossoms growing out from between the roots of a big tree. They're talking to the flowers as they pluck at them.

"Well, what do we have here? Never seen *you* growing anywhere in the realm before . . ."

Their voice is low and rough, like gravel when my shoe scrapes across it. The person stands up and holds the purple blossoms to the sky, examining them. I can't see their face yet, but they're old, with long white hair that sticks up wildly in all directions. They're wearing pants and a long cape, both a dark green color that blends into the foliage all around. I squint and make out two brown cloth sacks tossed over their shoulder.

"Hmm, are you something that can help with rashes?" they mutter to the flowers. "Perhaps calm fevers and soothe spots? Or are you something less kind, something that might make bones ache or a head swim with dizziness?"

A head swim with dizziness? If this person knows about heads and dizziness, could they know something about heads and *fog*?

I have to find out—it can't hurt just to ask, right? I step around the corner quietly, not wanting to startle them. Older people never seem to like being surprised. I'm trying to decide how to sneak up without actually being sneaky when the person stuffs a whole purple blossom into their mouth.

Thinking about the different kinds of poisonous plants you can find in Vancouver, I can't help but blurt out, "Are you sure those flowers are safe to eat?"

The old person startles and spins to face me. "Aaagh! What? How? Who?" Their mouth is still full so it all comes out like *aaarh wha wo hoo?*

I walk up to them, feeling bad. "Sorry! I didn't mean to scare you." Now that I'm closer, I can see the person is an old man, with a wild white beard that matches the wild white hair. Two horns stick out of his forehead, like a bull's or antelope's. "Are you okay?"

He swallows and stares at me suspiciously. "A mortal! How did you come to be here?" As he asks this, his cape falls open from his front, showing his middle.

It's clear as crystal.

Shennong the Medicine King?

"You're supposed to be dead," I whisper.

"I am?" Shennong grunts and shifts his two bags onto his other shoulder. They're just like in his myth, one for medicine and one for poison. "And yet you're here with me. Does that mean *you're* also dead?"

"No, I—" Could I have drowned in the Weak Water? I pat myself all over, as though that tells me anything in a realm of magic. "I feel too normal to be dead."

He shakes his head and scoffs. "A bigger clue is that this isn't Diyu. Trust me, you would know—the true underworld is nothing but fire and misery."

"But how can you still be alive?" I definitely know Shennong's myth. "The last thing you ate was that intestine-ripping poison."

"Death might not necessarily be death as you believe it to be. I merely faded and then reappeared elsewhere. I've been in this part of the world since my time in the realm of Zhen came to an end." Suddenly, the god grunts and makes a face, and we both look at his middle. The purple blossom is breaking up into tiny pieces inside his see-through stomach. They crash around like sharp-edged plastic confetti.

"Ugh," Shennong groans.

"Does it hurt?"

"Well, it sure doesn't feel good." He takes a cup of covered tea from beneath his cape and drinks. A second later, the tea swirls into his stomach and washes it clear. Shennong grunts again, bends down to pluck more of the purple blossoms, and drops them into his poison bag. "I'll call that gee-sick-bohl-li—'purple glass'—and note it as something that doesn't heal at all."

He starts walking down the alley, ignoring me. I walk with him, not ready to let him go yet. I can't believe I found the Medicine King! "Can I ask you some questions?"

"No." He gives me a grumpy look. "I don't have time to be followed. How did you get to be here, anyway?"

"I fell through the Weak Water. My friends and I are trying to get to Kunlun Mountain. I have to stop a demon named Chaos who wants to destroy all of Zhen with a flood."

Shennong snorts but doesn't stop walking. "Well, *that* seems a rather selfish goal."

"Are you still looking for new medicines?"

"Of course, that's what I do."

"How do you know you haven't found them all?"

He waves me off, impatient. "There's always new medicines to be found. Always new ways to heal that we've yet to discover. All right, time to go find your friends and let me get back to my task." He stops at a shrub grown over with yellow berries. He plucks one and swallows it. We both watch as the yellow berry shows up in his clear middle and begins to roll around. A second later, the berry seems to melt and his stomach is coated with soft-looking golden cream.

"Whoa, that's so cool," I say.

Shennong shakes a handful of the yellow berries into his medicine bag. "This one will be nwuahng-ooh-goh-dwoi—'warm stomach berry.' For easing stomachaches."

He starts walking again.

"What if there *aren't* new ways to heal?" I ask, keeping up. "How can you be so sure we don't already know them all?"

"Because. It's been thousands of years and I'm still finding new medicines, aren't I? And new medicines mean new paths. Look, this is new, too." He stops in front of some pale green ground cover that's growing across the path. He bends over, picks one of the tiny green leaves, and eats it. He stands up and we watch the leaf calmly make its way through him.

"Such instant relaxation of the mind. I'll call it moong-twoi—'dream grass.'" He tosses several leaves into his medicine bag, then passes me some. "For your next rest-less night. Now be off. I'm a busy man with no time for questions."

I hold the dream grass in my palm, careful to not crush its velvety softness. "Okay, but do you have any-thing that *wakes up* your mind? Or more, like, helps with depression by freeing someone's mind from it?"

Shennong sighs hugely. "If I help you with this final question, will you leave me alone?"

I nod. "Promise."

"Fine. Let me think. Hmm, depression. A sickness of the mind. When the world loses color and meaning for too long."

Hope flutters. "You have medicine for it?"

"No, I don't, I'm sorry." He shifts his bags over onto his other shoulder. "I don't believe I can give you any medicine that will fix such a sickness. Goodbye." Shennong heads down the path again.

"Wait!" I shove the dream grass into my back pocket and run to catch up, disappointment crushing. "How can you have no medicine? You're the *Medicine King*! You said you would help!"

He shrugs, not slowing down. "Not all sicknesses can be cured by medicine. And sometimes not even by magic."

"What do you mean magic might not work?" Desperation makes my voice climb. "Magic's supposed to save Mom!"

"Look, I'm sorry to hear your mother is sick. But sometimes medicine is only part of the solution."

"So what's the rest?"

"Life energies *can* be rebalanced with medicine, but sometimes rebalancing must also come from within. Only your mother can do that."

The Medicine King sounds way too much like Marilla. Telling me I need to be like water for Mom instead of trying to bash my way through her being sick. But even gods can be wrong, too, right? Erlang once had some messed-up ideas about mortals. Gonggong shouldn't have ever tried to knock down Mount Buzhou. Even Shennong himself made the mistake of ingesting a poison so strong he had to change realms. How can magic (when it isn't slowly being stolen by a demon, anyway) not always be enough?

Now Shennong finally stops walking. He studies me more carefully. "You've come to stop a demon's flood, so you say? To do this, you will have to be at your strongest. Your life energy must be in balance, your qi healthy. It means you need to heal this conflict of yours."

"You mean how I'm still trying to fix Mom?"

He nods. "To defeat Chaos, you must trust yourself. And to do that, you must first trust your mother."

"I don't understand."

"To do is to understand." Shennong opens up his medicine bag and hands me what might be the universe's most beautiful fruit, a teeny tiny apple-like fruit with rainbow skin. "This is a fruit from the heng-ho tree. To help lead you back to where you need to go. Good luck."

He heads down the alley. Still holding the heng-ho fruit, I watch him disappear.

Trust your mother.

I'm not supposed to do anything at all? When my chance to fix everything is so close?

I shake my head, sure the god is still wrong (just as he's wrong about magic not always working), and bite into the tiny rainbow fruit. Hopefully, Shennong's at least right about helping me get out of here.

The fruit tastes of roses and raspberries, of light and sun. I chew and swallow. A second later my ears *open*, and I hear things I never noticed before. The squeaking of a rock as my sneaker pushes it deeper into the ground. The tiny feet of an insect crawling along a vine. The soft lapping of a wave of the Weak Water overhead. There's also a kind of breathless gasping that I automatically think is coming from me, since it's such a familiar sound. But it's not me at all, which is creepy because I can't tell what *is* making it. Then I wonder if it's one of the others, and I start walking fast out of the alley, trying to get closer to the sound.

"Hey, I'm here!" I yell as I leave the alley and turn back into the streets. "Where are you? Can you hear me?"

The gasping breathlessness keeps coming, and I walk even faster, *really* hoping it's not some awful mythical monster I'm chasing after. Like the jiangshi, vampires who hunt the living to steal their qi (which I definitely don't need). Or a shui gui, the ghost of a drowned person who hangs out around water looking for someone to haunt. *(Don't think about the watery purple sky right above you!)*

Deep in my ears, I hear the gasping sound start to smooth out and become regular breathing. When I hear my name a second later, it's such a loud shout that I jump into the air.

Astrid! Where are you?

It's Sae! They sound so close I can't believe they're not right here beside me. But it's the heng-ho at work, carrying Sae's shout over to me. Now I just need to go find them, wherever they are.

I run in the direction of the shout. "Sae!" I call out, even though I'm pretty sure they still can't hear me. I wonder how they found another way down here.

Astrid, answer if you're here!

"I'm here!" I keep running through the streets. I'm starting to wheeze and I tighten my grip on my clarinet. The streets turn and turn. Terra-cotta everything blurs and rushes by. I take a final corner and see the immortal.

"Sae!" I yell as I run over. I'm so happy to see them that I nearly knock them over with my clumsy hug.

They laugh and hug me back. "You weren't supposed to get off the travel cloud *quite* that early."

Their voice is at normal volume now; the heng-ho fruit must have worn off.

I let go and look down the street. "The others didn't come with you? How did you find a way in?" I can't miss how Sae looks more drained than ever, Chaos still stealing their qi. How much longer before they completely fall under the spell of grim magic?

"They're waiting on the shore," Sae says. "We were close enough that Erlang was able to get them there on his own. And I got here by jumping into the Weak Water after you."

My mouth drops open. "You *jumped*? Weren't you scared?" Now I understand why they were gasping before; they were still catching their breath after coming out of the water.

"I was terrified." Sae blinks, thinking back, and the shadow of their old fear rises in their eyes. "I kept imagining the Dragon Prince beneath the surface waiting to imprison me again. But then I thought about *you* being imprisoned, and so I jumped." Now they grin, and there's a new lightness in their eyes that pushes the fear shadow back. "I'm glad you're all right."

I throw my arms around them in another hug, happy for that new lightness. "I'm glad you are, too. Maybe jumping into water from now on will only get easier."

"You know, I think it might be."

I step back. "Thanks for finding me. I was getting worried about staying lost."

Sae grins again. "Well, we still need you to stop the prophecy. You go down, we all go down."

"Funny. Okay, so let's get out of here! What is this place, anyway?"

Sae glances around our terra-cotta world. "I can't be sure, as Zhen has many ancient sunken cities. And I never knew there was one beneath the Weak Water. But they're all places of the past now, no longer places for the living."

"That reminds me—Shennong's here!"

"Ah, the Medicine King." Sae nods. "He *has* been dead for centuries. I suppose he's come to exist in this part of the world, then. Is he still gathering medicines?"

"Sure is." I hold out the heng-ho fruit with my single bite out of it. "He gave this to me to help lead me out. It's how I heard you."

"A heng-ho fruit!" Sae studies it, thinking. "The Red River is nearby. You can't hear it down here, but perhaps if we had some help . . ."

We each take bites of the tiny rose-flavored fruit, finishing it off. In a second the rushing sound of water fills my ears, as loud as a waterfall.

"Can you hear that?" Sae asks.

I nod.

We run as fast as we can while making sure my asthma doesn't get too bad (Sae left my backpack with my inhalers with the others). The streets twist and turn and seem directionless—only the sound of the Red River promises we're going the right away. Soon the streets start to feel more like hills, and I have to slow to a walk.

"How much farther do you think?" I whisper, my breaths whistling.

"Better not be much at all," Sae says. "The effects of the heng-ho fruit will start to wear off soon. We *are* getting closer to the surface, which is a good sign."

A few minutes later we end up at a wide door. It's heavy, the terra-cotta of it a deep orange. There's a peephole, too, its cover a small ornamental lion head also made out of terra-cotta. I slide it across and press my eye to the peephole.

Sun. The outdoors. Relief washes over me. "This is it!"

"About time." Sae tests the door's bolt, but it's rusted through and doesn't budge. They sift through their basket and pull out a silver blade of grass. They draw it across the bolt and the old metal drops to the floor with a heavy *thunk*. The ancient peephole cover falls off at the same time, the terra-cotta lion head rolling onto my foot. I pick it up (another souvenir, why not?) and shove it into my jeans pocket.

I yank the door open and we rush through.

NINETEEN

We come out onto a high grass-covered ledge. Trees encircle it to block the view, some of the tallest trees I've ever seen. Everything is more white than green, like we're caught in the middle of a snowstorm. Which way to go to find the others?

Before I can ask Sae, Howl bursts out from around the trees, barking as he runs. He hits my leg with his head and I scrub his neck and ears. Golden armor or not, he's acting just like how Bear acts when Jasper comes home from school. He bounds over and jumps at Sae in greeting.

"Astrid!"

A black shape darts through the grass. A second later, Marilla leaps at me, her paws squeezing around my neck. Cat or not, I'm pretty sure my sister's never hugged me this hard before, and just like that, everything between us feels okay again (I guess a near-death experience will do that). I squeeze her back, as much as I can really squeeze a cat without hurting them. "Marilla!"

"I thought you were never coming back."

"Surprise!"

"I was really scared, okay?" Marilla sounds like she might actually cry (except that she's a cat, so she can't). "You're a really bad swimmer in *normal* water."

She's right.

"Thanks for the reminder."

I keep hugging her, my own throat going tight. For a second, I wish that I could talk to her once more about the peach. But she'd only get mad all over again, and I've already been missing her too much. I only let go when she pokes her claws into my neck.

She jumps down to the white-green grass. "So what's at the bottom of the Weak Water?" she asks. "Erlang says no one ever knew."

"An old sunken city. And I talked to Shennong!"

"You got to meet the *Medicine King*?" She remembers this myth, too, then. "Is his stomach really see-through?"

"Yes. It was gross but also cool."

Erlang strides up and hands me my backpack. He claps me on the back. "I never thought a mortal could survive a fall into the Weak Water, but I'm glad it was you. We wouldn't have gotten across without your power to help us, either. Chaos would be right to be afraid of you—and a fool if not."

The mention of Chaos makes everything rush back. Still wheezy, I use my rescue inhaler and look around, trying to see through the trees. A mix of feelings race around my stomach, from fear to excitement to wonder. Once Kunlun Mountain was just a story and a painting; now it holds the key to the world.

I put away my inhaler and clarinet. I take the dream grass and terra-cotta lion head from my pocket and put those safely into my backpack. I check to make sure *A Handbook of Ancient Chinese Myths* is still safe in the front pocket (it is).

"How close are we to the mountain now?" I ask.

"This way," Sae says.

I slide my backpack on and follow the others as they go back around the trees. The grass-covered ledge we were on widens, the trees thin out, and the realm opens up.

Kunlun Mountain fills the sky. It's so huge the rest of Zhen seems to slip away from it, the same way the entire world becomes all ocean when you're standing at its shore. For a second, I'm confused about where the divine cloud cover went, before I realize we're inside it.

Right away it's easy to tell that Chaos's power is strongest here, the mountain his new home. Every part of it appears blanketed with snow, the thick heavy kind that becomes deadly avalanches.

I blur my eyes. I want to see *through* the grim magic, see Kunlun the way it really is—and look once more.

Huge slabs of gleaming purple rock make up the mountainside. Earth-brown ribbons coil along its surface (walking trails!). Cliffs are carved out of ivory, and honey-colored boulders sit here and there. Forests pop up in between, these giant clumps of both emerald-green and ocean-blue trees. Roofs of dozens of different palaces peek out, all shining gold and glowing jade. I imagine nine-tailed tigers, fancy black peacocks, deer that can speak roaming all over.

A stream of water runs down one side of the mountain, gathering speed as it nears the base. Afternoon sun winks off the water so that the air glitters with diamond droplets. It's the Red River—we've followed it back to its source here at Kunlun.

I tilt my head up and see Kunlun's peak. A thin crown of clouds sits atop it.

I blink and everything goes white again. But my heart is still full—I can't believe I'm actually here. *Mom, we'll remember every detail to tell you—so that you'll be able to see it, too.*

I look down at the ground where the Red River is gushing wildly across it. Here it's not even the color of pink lemonade but straight-up milk—too much grim magic. The white of it pools outward, over soil gone as colorless as the surface of the moon.

"Can you see the parasol trees from here?" I ask Erlang. We're close enough now that even with Chaos stealing his magic, his third eye might still be able to see.

Erlang tilts up his helmet and gazes upward. He grins and points at the peak. "Right there! A grove of trees with leaves as big as a warrior's hand. Where all the wood bends without breaking."

"Anything around that might be a weapon?" Sae asks, also looking.

Erlang shakes his head and lowers his helmet. "Not that I can see. But I also don't know what to look for." He gestures to the valley down below with his spear. "That's our path to the mountain. That dry part of land between the shore of the Weak Water and where the Red River turns toward the rest of the realm."

We run down the chalky-white slope of the ledge. We hit the bottom and keep running, our feet stirring up white valley dust. The sun's getting lower and the need to hurry gnaws at me like hunger. Not only is Chaos still growing stronger and the rest of Zhen weaker, I bet it's a lot harder trying to find a mysterious object in the dark.

We're halfway across when a low shout rings across the valley.

I skid to a stop. "Anyone else hear that?"

Everyone else stops, too. Sae frowns and turns toward the Red River. "It came from downriver."

Erlang flicks up his helmet and unveils his third eye. "Let me."

More shouts come. They're muffled, sounding far away.

"The sound of the river makes it hard to hear," Marilla says, ears flattening as she listens. "I can't tell what the shouts are saying."

"Those aren't just shouts." Erlang covers his eye and grabs his spear. "Those are commands. It's Chaos and the Dragon Prince—and they've brought the Dragon King's army."

Dread slams into my chest. Our painting of *The Eight Immortals Cross the Sea* flashes into my head, the silk threads of the Dragon Prince and the king's army tumbling Sae deep into the water.

"No," Sae breathes as the Dragon Prince fills their head, too. They see the Red River but also the East Sea. They might have dived into water for me, but to face this part of their nightmare is something else.

"But Chaos is supposed to be at Mount Buzhou!" I say. "Doesn't he want to finish what Gonggong started?"

"Perhaps the demon is writing a new myth," Erlang growls. "There are sky pillars other than Mount Buzhou, but there's only one Kunlun Mountain."

"We should have known." Sae now sounds cold with anger. "Kunlun is where the realm's gods and goddesses spend their time when they're away from their homes. They're who witnessed Gonggong's humiliating fall to Earth all that time ago."

The commands of the Dragon King's army grow louder, the noise swelling over the rumbling of the river.

"The prince shouldn't even be awake," Marilla insists. "In 'Sleeping Beauty,' the kingdom all wakes up at the same time."

"He's still asleep," Sae says, "but it's a sleep controlled by Chaos. His actions won't be his own. Chaos chose him for this because he knows what I fear."

"Another mind game," Erlang says. "It won't work."

"Can we truly be so sure? We believed Chaos would be at Mount Buzhou, didn't we?"

The king's army rumbles closer. Water splashes sharply along with the high clang of armor. The ground trembles.

"It'll be okay," I say. It has to be. We're not done yet. "We just have to get to the parasol trees before Chaos can break the mountain. C'mon, let's go!"

Sae shakes their head. "You and Marilla go. Find the weapon to beat Chaos. Erlang and I will come find you afterward."

"What? We can't just leave you here." No one said we

were supposed to split up. The dread pounds and drums. "Marilla and I can fight, too! You need us now that your magic is weak."

"You can transmute me!" Marilla does the Bruce Lee kick. "How about a giant mermaid to attack from below? Or a huge hawk from above!"

"Sae's right," Erlang says. "Our magic may be weakened, but we're still awake to fight. And Astrid needs to get to the top of the mountain."

"They're here." Sae's eyes are locked in the direction of the milky river. From Erlang's side, Howl begins to growl.

Chaos appears first, his physical form finally finished. The demon's serpent body uncoils into the air, monstrous as his bottom half slithers fast through the water. His bright red hair is exactly as it was in my dream. His copper face winks in the sun as he grins, long forked tongue lashing.

The Dragon Prince is beside him. Silver armor drapes his body, the sword in his hand a matching silver; a long black cape streams from his shoulders. His black hair is wound into a bun on the top of his head, and his empty staring eyes are completely white. He's riding a creature that has a coat of thick emerald scales. Sawlike teeth fill an oversized mouth. A tail made up of armored plates waves through the water like a propeller.

"A panlong," I whisper. The mythological water dragon isn't known for working with the Dragon Prince—Chaos must have woken it up just for this.

Next, the Dragon King's army appears. Made up of human-sized shrimps and crabs, dozens of shell-armored bodies march as one. Sword-sharp claws and pincers cut through the water and glint in the air. Their eyes are just as creepily white and empty as the prince's.

I never thought a bunch of shrimps and crabs could be scary (just delicious; they're in all of Dad's favorite dishes from Mandarin Garden), but now I know how wrong I was.

Chaos starts to rise out of the water. He uncoils faster and faster, ten feet tall now, twenty feet, fifty feet. Soon he's as tall as our ten-story apartment building back home, over a hundred feet of evil serpent. Wet smoke-gray scales gleam, seeming as strong as huge plates of steel. Chaos's copper-mask face is full of glee as he peers down at us. His red hair blazes from around his head like something on fire.

"Say goodbye to Zhen, you fools!" he hisses. He lifts his tail and brings it crashing down into the river. An enormous tower of water billows up into the air, curls white at the top, then cascades back to earth with a thunderous roar.

The Red River swarms up over its shores and drags all of us into the water.

"Ooof!" I fall down hard on my tailbone. Marilla streams past me, yowling, and I reach out and grab her by a paw. She latches onto my arm and starts climbing up.

"Ouch, your claws!" I yell.

"Sorry!" she yells back as she clutches onto my shoulder.

Still on my butt, I look all the way up until my neck hurts and I'm squinting against the sun. Chaos is just ahead of us in the water, his copper face high above and grinning down—I can tell he wants us to know that he's having fun. His orange-red coal eyes burn into mine.

"Assssstrid!" His forked tongue flicks. "How nicccce to be meeting again. Now, didn't I warn you to leave?"

"I'm not going anywhere!" I shout, even as a pang shoots through me at the idea of home. "Not until you leave first!"

He whips his tail down into the river again. *Crash!*

I cough and sputter as whitened water roars down. Chaos and I keep staring at each other, and an icy fear fills the pit of my stomach. It lodges in my chest like a bad cold, digs into my brain like the worst kind of news. Because his burning-coal eyes hold a promise, which is that he's going to beat us all—end us and the entire realm. The excitement in them is terrible to see, and a sense of doom washes over me just like the river water did.

"Chaos!" Sae stands beside Marilla and me. Their blue silk robe is soaked, but they still somehow look majestic and powerful. The sight helps push away my sense of doom. "End this now, and the emperor might still have mercy."

The serpent giggles, then hisses. He uncoils yet another foot taller. "Lan Caihe, oh, how I look forward to desssss-stroying you as well."

Sae whips around to face me. Their expression is cold and set. "Astrid, get back! Hurry!"

I start backing away, crawling toward dry land. Rocks in the riverbed dig into my palms, but I keep going. Just past Chaos, I see the Dragon Prince getting closer. Eyes as blank as snow, his sword shining and sharp. The panlong plods forward, each step shaking the earth.

Erlang strides through the water, sword drawn. His damp red cape billows in the wind. Howl is at his side, already in attack mode and growling loudly, his wet fur all raised. "Mind if I call you Gonggong?" Erlang bellows up at Chaos. "Or is that just a painful reminder of how you once lost like no other god has ever lost before?"

Chaos's tongue darts out, spitting, and he twists high into the air. His eyes glow hot. "Give me Asssssstrid! Give me the mortal!"

"I don't think so, you puny snake!" I yell, finally getting to my feet. The Dragon King's army is right behind the Dragon Prince, pincers and claws already snapping at the air. I watch as Sae and Erlang begin moving backward. Howl stays on guard, growling as Chaos's head slithers back and forth in the air.

"Oh my gosh, why are you goading him?" Marilla leaps from my shoulder to the ground. "He's a puny snake like King Kong is a puny gorilla!"

Sae and Erlang reach us.

"Astrid, take this." Sae pulls the Scroll of Chaos from their straw basket. It's still dry because of its protective layer of wax. "If there's anyone left awake on the mountain to stop you, it'll prove why you're there. And Kunlun is Zhen's most sacred, so even the smallest creatures may still have some magic."

Panic stings my eyes and I stare at Sae. All my doubts roll through me, the biggest one still being: What if I'm just not good enough?

"Remember," they say, watching my face, "it's okay to be scared."

Fear is why there is such a thing as bravery.

I take the scroll from their hand. "Make the Dragon Prince get his own clappers, okay?"

Sae smiles. "We'll meet you and Marilla at the top."

I look over at Erlang, remembering his fear of never being strong again. "Thanks for fighting Chaos here to give me the chance to fight him up there."

"You're welcome." Erlang glares up into the sky. "The serpent won't have it easy. Now go!"

Sae digs into their flower basket. They slip yao grass into their mouth and a second later their hoe is a long gold sword. Another mouthful of yao grass and their basket becomes a gold bow-and-arrow set that hangs from their side.

Next they grab their famous jade clappers. Bright green gemstone flashes in the air—a call to the Dragon Prince. The clappers ring out, the sound as deep as a gong.

"Dragon Prince!" Sae's yell ripples out in the direction of the Red River as they turn and face their fear. They sound their clappers again and another deep *gong* echoes across the water. "Are these what you want?"

The prince sneers, his pale eyes emptier than ever, and charges. The king's army surges with him, giant claws and pincers clacking and snapping.

Chaos's serpent body lunges, thick as a tree trunk and

seemingly endless. Full of power. "The realm isssss mine!" he hisses.

Erlang rushes into the swirling milk-colored water to meet him, the warrior's yell a roar. His triple-pointed spear glints with the sun; his bow and arrow gleam at his hip. Howl races alongside, teeth bared.

The sight of the battle paints itself into my mind: *Clash at Red River.*

Marilla and I run for Kunlun Mountain.

TWENTY

We reach the mountainside a couple of minutes later, nearly crashing into it since we're going so fast. Marilla slaps at the rock excitedly with her paws. "We're here, we're here!"

"Keep going," I huff out, "until they can't see us anymore."

We circle around, stopping when the sound of the river drops to a low gurgle. I hug the white wall of the mountain and try to catch my breath.

"Do you want your inhaler?" Marilla asks.

"I'm okay." I step back and slowly look all around. It's like we've stepped right into Mom's painting. Or like her painting's come to life. Both feel right. "Wow," I whisper. "Look at this place."

My sister spins in a circle, full of new awe. "I am!"

"I mean *really* look, Marilla. Look through the grim magic so you really see."

She slows. Her cat eyes widen. "It's the world of all our stories."

The mountainside glows, a giant lavender gem. Gold and bronze mosses climb between patches of blue grass and decorate the top of small boulders. Frilly orange-pink mushrooms line branches and trunks. A nearby tree offers Ping-Pong ball–sized fruit that looks exactly like giant pearls.

I crouch down and touch a dropped fruit beneath the tree. It cracks open and something like oil spills out onto the dirt. Instantly, a green seedling unfurls and starts to grow.

A grin spreads across my face. I wonder what kind of medicine this is and how it heals. If it actually works more by magic than medicine. How maybe they can almost be the same thing.

I have to find Xiwangmu's garden. Somewhere on this mountain is the peach that's going to save Mom. Shennong has to be wrong about magic not always being enough.

Marilla leaps onto a cloud of golden moss. "This stuff smells like perfume! The *expensive* kind at the mall I'm not supposed to touch."

I dive into my own golden cloud. The fragrance wraps me up and it'd be so easy to forget what I have to do. It'd be so easy to think about nothing at all . . .

I sit up, pulse now racing. The world shifts back to white—Chaos's world—and I scramble to my feet. *This place is Chaos's now. Full of tricks.*

"Marilla, get up, we have to go." I slip the scroll into my back pocket. "We have to start climbing."

My sister—up to her cat chest in gold moss—jumps up. She shakes herself, like she's waking up. "Right. So where do we start?"

We walk farther around the base of the mountain until we reach a path. Its dirt is white now, but Marilla scratches at it with her paw, and beneath the grim magic, it's the same earthy brown I saw earlier from the ledge. The walking trail winds up the mountain before it disappears behind some white shrubs (which are supposed to be blue).

"This way," I say.

Marilla's ears flick as she also gazes up at the path. "Are you going to be okay with your asthma? This is kind of steep."

I start heading up, convincing her—and myself—as I go. "Every path is going to be like this. But there'll be parts where it'll go flat, so those will be easy. And I'll use my inhaler if I need to."

She pounces ahead of me to take the lead. "I'll help you control your pacing."

"Thanks, Coach Xu." I breathe deep and slow to keep my asthma under control. It's always hardest going uphill.

We climb. Now that we've gone far enough around the

mountain that we can't see or hear the Red River anymore, there's no way to tell how the others are doing. All we can do to help them is keep going. I move as fast as I can, ignoring the dull ache already building in my chest. Marilla doesn't make any jokes about my speed, even though we both know I'm the one holding us back. Maybe before I fell into the Weak Water, she might have joked about it. Sometimes she stops for me to take a break, but sometimes we stop just because of Kunlun.

Some of the strange and beautiful things we blur our eyes to see:

A bird's nest full of orange eggs dotted with the constellations in silver.

A pond lined with luminous nuggets of gold.

A rainbow waterfall.

The sun drops closer to the horizon. At one point, I take a puff of my rescue inhaler. I can only use it a few more times in the next few hours; any more than that could lead to a bad reaction.

"Maybe we should stop for a real break," Marilla says as she lopes along ahead of me, black tail swishing through the air.

"No, we can't," I say over the raspy sound of my breathing.

"You sound bad."

"Just keep going!"

We walk around a huge white boulder (which is actually a boulder of jade) and nearly smash into a gate on the other side.

"Guess it's break time now, no matter what." Marilla stops extra quick because of her cat feet, and I nearly trip over her. "What's a gate doing in the middle of the path?"

Still catching my breath, I go to shake the bars even though I can tell they're not going to budge. "We have to get past. We'll lose too much time trying to find a different path to the top." Remembering Sae's hope that not all of the mountain was asleep, I call through the bars. "Hello? Can someone help us?"

"Here, I'll do it, you're all wheezy." She slips her head through the bars (she fits, unlike me). "Hellooo, is anyone around?" she bellows. "We need someone to let us through this gate, please!" She does this for an entire minute before plonking herself down on my sneaker. "Got another idea?"

I shake my head, suddenly feeling close to tears. "We have to go back and find another path." All that climbing and running, wasted . . .

"Wait, someone's coming!" Marilla jumps off my foot and looks through the jade bars. "Hello! We're here!"

I look through the bars but don't see anyone. "Who are you talking to?"

"I can't tell yet, I only heard them."

A black-spotted gray cat strolls up to the gate and meows at us.

Marilla stares at the cat. "*You're* the one talking to us?"

Even the smallest creatures will have some magic. "Are there more of you not under Chaos's spell?"

The cat meows again.

"She says she can't understand you, Astrid, only me." My sister widens her cat eyes. "Like, this is really cool but also really freaky, don't you think?"

"How come she understands you but not me?" I ask. "You're just speaking, you know, human talk."

"She says my words turn into meows in her head. Which makes sense since *her* meows turn into words in *mine*. So that's how we're talking."

"Can you ask her how we can get by the gate?"

More meows from the cat.

"She says it's one of the Outer Gates and only gods and goddesses are allowed to pass. The guardian who's supposed to be here isn't, and they have the key."

"Can she tell us if there's another way around?"

Marilla asks, and I'm pretty sure the cat gives me a

side-eye as she meows back an answer (I make sure not to side-eye back).

"She says yes!" my sister exclaims. "*Buuut* that the cats here on the mountain only share information with other cats. They don't trust any other beings here, not even gods or goddesses. I can get past, but you can't."

I frown. Marilla getting to the top of Kunlun Mountain without me won't stop the prophecy. There must be something that will convince the cat to help. We exchange looks for a moment before it hits me.

"I know!" I say. "If we tell her the story of why cats don't trust anyone else, will she let us pass?"

"What are you talking about?"

"The myth of all the animals racing one another! The one about why the cat isn't a part of the Chinese zodiac."

Marilla's whiskers droop. "I don't know that story well enough anymore to tell it. And I have to be the one to do it since she can't understand you."

"You can read it to her from the handbook."

She cat-grins. "The book! I forgot. Okay, hold on." She asks the cat, and the cat turns to look at me, her large eyes more curious than anything now. Hope glimmers, like a peek of sun through fog. She finally meows a reply.

"She agrees!" Marilla says.

Phew. I take out *A Handbook of Ancient Chinese Myths*, open it to the right page, and place it on the ground for Marilla to read.

The Great Race

More than a thousand years ago, when the land of China was still very new, the Jade Emperor decided to hold a glorious banquet at his royal palace. He invited all the animals of the earthly realm, wishing to meet as many as would come to Kunlun Mountain. He also offered a prize: The first twelve animals to arrive would be forever celebrated by becoming an animal in the Chinese zodiac.

Two good friends, Cat and Rat, soon got their invitations. Now, neither was a good swimmer, but both really wanted to win. They agreed to ask their friend Ox if they could ride on his back when he crossed the river to the palace. Ox, who was very strong, didn't mind at all.

And so Cat and Rat made the first part of the journey over land together, and then waited for Ox at the shore of the river. Once Ox arrived, the two friends hopped on his back and Ox started to swim across. Because Ox was so strong, the three were the first to reach the other side.

Just as they were about to step onto shore, Cat turned to ask Rat if he needed help getting down. But before he could, Rat pushed Cat off Ox so that Cat fell back into the river!

Ox—who didn't know that Cat was no longer on his back—finished swimming with just Rat. As soon as they reached land, Rat jumped off Ox and ran ahead to the Jade Emperor's palace. And this is how Rat won the race and why he is the first animal in the zodiac.

As for Cat, being a poor swimmer, he had to watch from the river as other animals swam past him. These would be the other eleven winning animals:

Ox.

Tiger.

Rabbit.

Dragon.

Snake.

Horse.

Goat.

Monkey.

Rooster.

Dog.

Pig.

Some people say Cat drowned and never made it to the Jade Emperor's banquet. But others say he did go, to explain to the Jade Emperor what happened, only for the emperor to turn him away and reward Rat anyway.

Today, this is why cats hate water. It's also why cats will always find the time to chase rats. But here is yet one more truth, which is that cats today are one of the most revered animals of the world, zodiac or not. They own their own homes and roam them as royalty. Human servants serve them banquets every day, and cats are always held high over water so they never, ever have to swim.

I put the book away and peer down at the gray cat. "What's the verdict?"

Marilla asks the cat, and the cat—"Her name is Yu, by the way," my sister adds—whips her tail and meows. Yu slips out through the gate and steps onto the path. She crosses it and disappears into the nearby bushes.

Marilla dashes off after her. "We're supposed to follow. Sorry, Astrid, try to keep up!"

I do my best, but it's not easy. Yu and Marilla have cat bodies that can easily climb and leap while my human body is clumsier. I shove my way through tall shrubs (I don't try to see their real color, but their leaves ring faintly like bells when I touch them) and squeeze through cracks between giant boulders (made of stone that smells of smoke). Once every few seconds I catch sight of Marilla's black tail against the white of the world and it keeps me from getting completely lost.

Yu finally comes to a stop at the bottom of a moss-covered hill. The gray cat bounds up to a large rock halfway up. She looks up the hill and then turns back and meows at us.

"Are you sure?" Marilla calls out.

Meow.

"What is it?" I ask, huffing and puffing. The sun's slipped down some more, and panic keeps wanting to get closer. We haven't heard the Red River again, and though it's probably better to not know what's happening (since it won't change what I still have to do), it's super hard not imagining the worst.

"Yu says we're nearly back at the path," Marilla tells me. "We just go up the hill, past that big rock at the top, and then turn left."

"Thank you!" I shout to Yu.

"Yes, thanks!" my sister calls out. "And neither of us is Year of the Rat, in case you were wondering!"

The gray cat disappears from view, and we start climbing the hill. I'm still winded, so we decide not to run until we get to the top.

"You know, we'd still be stuck at the gate if you stayed human," I say. "I hope you're not feeling useless anymore just because you're a cat."

Marilla gives me her smug cat grin. "I'm not. *And* don't forget I scared away a whole bunch of nian by becoming a lion. Which is basically a cat, only bigger."

"See? I told you you'd be able to help."

"I wish I could help you all the way with fighting Chaos. Are you scared?"

I nod. "I wish I wasn't, even though I know it's natural."

"Well, I'm not worried." Her tail swishes from side to side. "Not with the way you have real magic in Zhen now."

"Maybe I'd feel better if I could use my clarinet to fight Chaos instead of whatever I'm going to find in the parasol trees. What if I can't figure out how to use it?"

"What if *you* matter even more than your clarinet does, though? You controlled the nian and kept the travel cloud in the sky all on your own, right? Sure, you used your clarinet, but you also did it without yao grass. I bet you'll be able to do something like that again."

The way Marilla says it seems so simple. So easy. It probably *does* seem that simple and easy to her—be like water and the universe will stay in balance. All that stuff that she believes. I never thought I'd ever want to be my sister—Marilla Godzilla, super athlete with super lungs— instead of Astrid Xu, clarinetist with very non-super lungs. But to be just as brave for one day would come in really handy right about now.

We finish climbing the hill and reach the rock (it's black) on top. An iron-type fence peeks out above it, enclosing whatever's behind the rock that we can't see. We turn left and we're back on the same path as before, but this time, there's no gate in our way.

"Oh, good, we didn't mess up Yu's directions," Marilla says. "Time to start running again?"

"Yep." I take a deep breath, getting ready.

The whiff of ripe fruit fills my nose.

Peaches.

TWENTY-ONE

I go still, my heart racing.

The Queen Mother of the West's garden! It must be right around here, with its immortal peaches inside.

Their scent seems everywhere. In my nose and drifting into my lungs. I imagine it like a soft invisible blanket, enveloping my entire body from head to toe. How very powerful their magic must be that Chaos can't even entirely put them under his spell. So powerful that anyone would be saved with a single bite.

I look around wildly, needing to find them. I rush back to the black rock, to the fence behind it.

"Where are you going?" Marilla asks, following me. "We have to go *that* way, not this way."

Ignoring her, I squish my way toward the back of the rock to see what's behind the fence.

A garden. Full of plants so lush it's hard to believe grim magic has put them to sleep, except that they've gone as white as the rest of the mountain (I blur my eyes to check, and the plants are a deep emerald green; the fence around them a brilliant shining gold).

The sweet scent of peaches comes in a thick wave.

"Astrid, c'mon—!"

I squeeze my way back out and face Marilla. "Can't you smell that? It's the immortal peaches! Xiwangmu's garden is right here behind this fence."

My sister just looks at me. "And we're going to ask her for one after you beat Chaos, remember? Now let's *gooo—*"

"I'm going to steal one, Marilla." I take a deep breath. "I know you don't want me to, but it really would be smarter to take one while we can. This is the only way to be sure to save Mom."

Marilla's cat mouth drops open. "You promised you wouldn't!"

"I never *promised*. I only said that it was just an idea."

"That's still lying!"

I can tell she's nearly as upset about me lying as she is about my stealing. "I'm sorry, but the peaches are right here! There's no way we can leave without one now."

She shakes her head fast. "I told you, this isn't how it's supposed to happen. This isn't being like water."

Sometimes I think I hate Bruce Lee.

"Okay, but what if being like water *is* why we've found the peaches on our own?" I ask. "Why can't *this* be the way we're meant to save Mom as long as we still stop the prophecy?"

"*Because it's just not, okay?* Because I'm too scared

to know that Mom might never get better, *okay?*"

The smell of peaches washes over me again, making me dizzy. Telling me to hurry. *It's just Marilla being scared about Mom again,* a voice that sounds like mine (except meaner) says in my head, *the only thing she can't be brave about. Even though she could if she really wanted to.*

"This is your last chance," I say. "If you're not going to help, I really will do it by myself." The meanness flares. "I've been trying to help Mom all on my own for a long time now, anyway."

Marilla's tail whips furiously. "You're not helping Mom! You just want to think you are, when you're actually as scared as me. But at least I can admit it."

"If I was scared like you, then I wouldn't be stealing an immortal peach from a goddess!"

My sister's whiskers tremble, like she's shivering. "Why do you have to be like this, Astrid? It's like you don't even care that we're always fighting now."

Something shivers inside my chest, too. "I care. But you're the one who never wants to talk about stuff anymore. Real stuff. Like Mom."

"*You're* the one who can't stop talking about how to fix her, which we both know we can't do!"

I take a step farther away from her and closer to the smell of the peaches. "Well, who even says we have to keep talking?" I was wrong about our last fight being our worst. "We never have to talk again!"

"Good!" Her cat face wobbles. "And you know what?" Now she's whispering, and her voice is thick the way it goes when she's trying not to cry. "Even if I knew this entire time that you were going to steal a peach, I still wouldn't have told Sae and Erlang. I was too scared Xiwangmu would punish you and you'd never talk to me again. And then I'd have to miss you, too, just like I miss Mom. But I don't think you'd miss me at all."

The shivering feeling clenches like a fist. Why can't she just understand? "Marilla, listen—"

"Are you really going to steal it?"

I stare at her, convincing myself she isn't as upset as she looks. Because she's supposed to be the brave one. I think about Mom finally free of fog. "I'm stealing it for all of us."

"Then I take it back. I *would* have told them if I'd known. And I wouldn't miss you a bit, either!" She turns and races away.

"Marilla!" I start going after her, but soon I stop. There's no point—she'll never let me catch up. I just hope she decides to go back down the mountain to wait for Sae and Erlang and Howl instead of staying around up here by herself.

I turn and follow the gold fence, looking for a gated

door—the fence isn't the kind you can climb. The outer edges of the garden poke through the bars as I run by and I blur my eyes to see their real colors—shrubs of pink, yellow branches, hand-sized flowers the color of old pennies. But no sign yet of the immortal peaches, even as their fragrance keeps wafting into the air.

Don't be stupid, Astrid. Think! The immortal peaches are Xiwangmu's most treasured prize. The most valued of all she grows. They could only be in one place in her famous garden, and that's right in the center.

I reach a gate and skid to a stop, breathing fast. I test the golden clasp and it swings open easily. For a second, I glance around, waiting for someone—or something—to leap out at me, yelling for a password or proof that I'm allowed in. But either the Outer Gate would normally be enough to stop any trespassers, or just the Queen Mother herself is, with all her magic. No one comes, though, and I step through, heart like a drum that pounds all the way up into my ears.

I enter the garden and rush toward its center. As I go, I notice the white of the world that is the garden isn't as solid as I first thought. It slowly fades in and out like a weakening light bulb. The real colors of the plants leak and crack through before fading again, as though someone's using an eraser and revealing everything while grim magic just swallows it up again. Chaos cast his spell over Xiwangmu's garden, but its magic is fighting back.

I run past shimmering silver mushrooms, a shrub growing bloodred heart-shaped fruit, herbs that cry black tears of juice. There's a plant with lip-shaped leaves (that laugh as I pass), and a flowering hedge that glows a glittery purple.

But I don't stop. I keep chasing after the sweet scent of ripe peaches. One second it seems as heavy as syrup gathered into the air, the next it seems barely there. I don't want to think about when their fragrance disappears forever, the demon's flood coming to wash all the peaches away for good.

My breath catches when I finally see the tree. It rises above the rest of the garden, the tallest tree around. Its crown is one of brilliant green leaves instead of hammered gold, and it's decorated with heavy rounded peaches instead of gems and jewels. The peaches pulse like they have hearts inside: pinks and golds and then white. Magic against magic.

I stop right beneath the tree, grinning even as I wheeze. *Mom, this is it.* I reach for one of the lowest peaches, and my hand trembles. The dooms of Chang'e and the Monkey King slide across my brain. I hear Shennong saying again that saving Mom isn't up to me. The echo of

Marilla yelling how she's too scared to want to know.

And I hear Mom, too.

Astrid, a peach taken this way won't taste sweet but sour. As bitter as poison. Perhaps it's not the gift you mean to give.

I lower my shaking hand, confused. I step back from the tree, half stumbling. My sneakers catch on something in the middle of the velvety green grass and I look down.

The Queen Mother of the West.

She's curled up on her side. Even under Chaos's spell she's super elegant, as though she's just emerged from Mom's painting and is still spun out of beautiful silk thread. But as one of the deities Chaos hates most and not as lucky as her garden, she's fully asleep under his spell.

I blur my eyes to see her for real. The ivory of her silk robe that's puddled on the ground. Dainty black silk slippers cover her feet. Bracelets of jade and gold circle her wrists and wrap around her ankles. Her silk robe hides her thick beast's tail, just like her heavy gold crown is doing its best to control her black and wild mane-like hair. If she were awake, she would flash teeth sharp enough that she might have ripped them straight from a tiger's mouth. Before she became a powerful goddess hundreds of years ago, she was a ferocious demon who lived in China's most remote mountains. She could have given up all the parts of her that were less human, but she chose not to. She loved those parts the most, she said.

I didn't know she would be here in her garden. I thought she would have already left for the palace along with the rest of the Jade Emperor's guests. I guess Xiwangmu was running late for the party.

I glance up at the immortal peaches again. They're so close! I'll never get this chance again.

I'd have to miss you, too, just like I miss Mom!

My heart twists. I stare down at the sleeping queen. I tell myself she looks more kind than beastly. From far away, the low hum of the Red River finally comes back—there's the distant clang of swords, of shouted commands. I have no idea how much time I still have before Chaos will be here.

I drop my backpack to the ground and unzip my clarinet case, hands clumsy and shaking. I put the instrument together and slip the case back into my bag.

You win, Marilla. I'll be like water the way you say I'm supposed to be.

My clarinet reed scrapes across the zipper of my backpack and splits apart.

"No," I whisper. A broken reed won't play anything that comes close to music. And it's my last.

I dig around the inside of my backpack, terrified. Maybe a spare slipped out and got stuck somewhere.

Maybe it's lying around in one of the little interior pockets—

I pull out small, velvety green leaves.

You having dream grass just when your last reed breaks? Marilla's voice says. *That's the flow of the universe, Astrid!*

I pop the leaves into my mouth.

The garden goes gauzy, like someone's dropped me into a snow globe and I'm looking out from behind the glass. There's nothing past it but blurry smears of color that fade in and out. The distant hum of the Red River goes even more distant, the way outside sounds do when you're indoors.

But Xiwangmu's treasured peach tree stays solid. And in this strange dream sleep, all its grim magic is gone.

"To enter a queen's sleep without her permission is a very foolish thing to do," a voice says.

I nearly yelp. I look over at the queen.

Xiwangmu also isn't blurry at all. She's as vivid and full of color as her tree of immortal peaches. Both are in the snow globe with me. She's even more majestic now that she's awake and on her feet. Which also makes her much more frightening. Her dark eyes say I won't escape without giving some kind of explanation.

I can't help but move back, remembering why she still has beast parts even after becoming a goddess.

"I'm here to help you," I say carefully. "But I also need *your* help."

"Oh?" She seems totally suspicious. (I get it. I didn't like Chaos invading my dream, either.) She points to my clarinet. "Is this your weapon from your own realm? What do you mean to do with it here in Zhen?"

"It's not a weapon, exactly." Out of nervousness, I nearly start explaining how it's just my clarinet for band class— even how it's just a rental—but then I think of all the things I've done with it so far here in Zhen. "Actually, I guess it is. And I've been using it to fight grim magic."

Her dark eyes flash. "How do you know of grim magic?"

I take the scroll from my jeans pocket and hold it out. "My name is Astrid Xu. I'm the one who broke the seal of the Scroll of Chaos. But I didn't know what it was, otherwise I wouldn't have, of course. And now I'm here to stop the prophecy."

The already-faint noise from the river goes away completely. The blinking colorful smears of the garden become solid.

Xiwangmu sighs with satisfaction. "I haven't been able to do that since Chaos started stealing my qi." She studies me. "And you are other-realm, which is why the demon has yet to steal yours. And why you are able to hold me in *your* spell now."

I'm about to tell her it's just Shennong's dream grass that pulled her into my sleep even as I entered hers, when I realize why everything's gone so still. "You've paused the prophecy!"

As a goddess, Xiwangmu hands out immortality. But as a wild demon, her ability was to stir up panic (a part of me thinks she'd be friends with Chaos if she'd stayed evil). She kept the ability the same way she kept her other demon parts, but now that she's good, she calms panic instead. Pauses it. She probably would have paused the prophecy earlier, but maybe Chaos's grim magic got to her first.

She nods. "But time is running out quickly, the prophecy very close to being fulfilled. I won't be able to hold it still forever."

"*Wow,*" I whisper. Sae and Erlang and Howl must be safe now, too, since whatever's happening in the Red River is also on hold. I look out at the stilled garden and think that home must be something like this, since Erlang is holding on to its time. But he's also growing weak . . .

Xiwangmu finally takes the scroll from my hand and reads it. When she's done, she rolls it back up and tucks it into the pocket of her silk robe.

"Welcome to the realm of Zhen, Astrid Xu." The Queen Mother smiles; there's a flash of tigerlike teeth. "Demon bringer but also the one who must save the realm. Now, how am *I* meant to help *you*?"

I take a deep breath. Like I'm about to step onstage in front of a huge audience to play the song that scares me the most.

"I'd like to ask for an immortal peach," I say. "It's for my mom back home. She's sick. Sae and Erlang said they would bring me here after I stop the prophecy, to ask for one as a reward."

"And yet I remain asleep. Chaos still lives and Zhen is in danger. Why are you asking for a reward before you've defeated him?"

"I was on my way to the top of Kunlun Mountain when I found your garden. I . . . actually came here to steal a peach, just in case you said no when I asked. But I couldn't do it." I hold out my clarinet with all its broken parts. "I went to wake you up from Chaos's spell to ask, but then I couldn't play. I had to enter your sleep of grim magic."

"Then you disturb me simply because of foolish intentions." Xiwangmu lifts a brow. "This is still my garden. I understood why you were here as soon as you stepped into my sleep. You are not the first to try to steal immortality. Or the first to be punished."

The snow-globe world spins. *Please don't exile me to the moon for all eternity. Please don't keep me trapped in a burning cauldron.* I chant this to myself like it can make a difference.

"*But,*" she continues, "you realized in time stealing was not the way. You came to the realm to help us and to fight Chaos. So, for giving Zhen a chance, you're free to continue your way to the top of the mountain."

My entire body slumps in relief. "Do you know if Sae and Erlang and Howl are still okay?"

"They are for now. Their magic and strength hold. But Chaos is continuing to grow. And the Dragon Prince won't give up the jade clappers again—he means to imprison Sae at the bottom of the East Sea once more."

I rush to the edge of the snow globe like it's something I can just step out of. Panic crashes inside me. "I have to get out of this dream! I've got to get to the top of the mountain. Where is Marilla? Is she okay?"

"There is a shortcut," Xiwangmu says. "It will take you directly to the parasol trees and the weapon they hold. But first . . ."

The Queen Mother reaches up and plucks a peach from her tree.

TWENTY-TWO

She holds out the magical fruit. In her hand the pinks and golds appear even richer. More true and real than anything else.

I slowly take the peach from her. My heart jumps and leaps, practically soars.

Chaos had only tricked me with the peach that he showed me in my dream. That peach had been soft as silk and the sweetest peach I thought I'd ever smell. But holding this one, I feel its warmth, radiating out like it's the sun itself. How it's ten times heavier than Chaos's peach. So full of magic. Already its sweetness stings my throat.

An immortal peach. This must be what superheroes feel like, able to do anything and save anyone. I'm holding infinity in my hand, but Mom doesn't even need infinity. The promise of a long and healthy and happy life is more than enough. Her fog, gone forever.

"I can really have this peach?" I ask Xiwangmu.

"Yes. And I don't gift my immortal peaches lightly. You might yet fail to beat Chaos, but what matters most in giving this to you is that you have chosen to try." She studies me closely again. "But I give you this peach with a single request."

"Okay." I'm already itching to tuck it safely into my backpack. And then once Mom's better, Marilla really won't be mad at me anymore. We'll never have to fight so badly again.

"That whatever truth it holds, you will accept that it's for the best."

I glance up. "What do you mean?"

"This peach might not be what you expect."

My heart dips and sways. "It doesn't promise Mom a super long life?"

"It might," the Queen Mother says, "but it might not. Our realms are not the same, and yet they are not entirely different; in between lies knowledge kept even from me."

"What about making her depression go away?" Now my heart's just hovering somewhere around my stomach, trembling all around.

"You can give it to your mother to see, just as you wish. But remember that my gift is meant to give you what you need. It might not be the same as what you want."

I touch the peach with a finger, wishing I could peek past its fuzzy, velvety skin and find out its secrets right this second. My heart's climbed up into my throat, stuck in there and stinging.

"You don't think it's going to save my mom, do you?" I whisper. "Because it's really up to Mom to find her own way to get better, along with the help of her doctors and medicines."

"It can be scary not being able to fix what we so badly want to," Xiwangmu says. "And yet, only by accepting this fear can one's qi be in balance. Inner harmony is never far from inner chaos, after all."

Trust Mom to trust myself. "What if I don't know how to be brave that way?"

She cocks her glamorous head. "Can one not be scared and brave at the same time?"

I know she's right. Now I just have to figure out that balance before I meet Chaos.

I pull Marilla's track pants from the bottom of my backpack, carefully wrap them around the peach, and nestle the whole thing safely on top of everything else. I zip up my bag securely and slide it back over my shoulders. "Thank you for the peach, even if doesn't work. And I promise I'll save Zhen."

"That is a promise you cannot make as much as you might wish to. But you can promise something else."

"I know—that I'll try."

Xiwangmu smiles. And even though I see the sharpness of her tiger teeth, reminding me of all her powers, she also reminds me of Mom, telling me she's proud no matter what happens.

"It's time to show you that shortcut," she says. "Because I cannot hold the prophecy still any longer."

"Wait!" I hold out my clarinet so she can see where it's all busted. "I can't wake you up for real to show me, remember?"

But the Queen Mother is already gone. So is her entire garden. I'm no longer there but instead at the top of Kunlun Mountain. The sky up here is a wide strip of clouds. The same clouds that formed a thin crown around the mountain's peak while looking up from down in the valley. It seemed so impossibly high up, and now I'm here.

I look out across the top of the mountain; everything around me is white as bone. Seeming of deep winter when it's actually spring. Forests are smothered with snow. Fields of grass and moss are bleached pale. Even the sunlight shining through the clouds seems more white than gold. I blur my eyes to try to see around me for real, but nothing happens—I can't see beneath Chaos's grim magic anymore. The demon is already more powerful and I shiver. For some reason I try to spot Marilla, look for a sign of black dashing along all the white, but there's nothing, and something inside me crumbles.

There's a grove of tall trees at one side. Their

ghost-white leaves are as big as a warrior's hand. I stare at their branches and instantly know that they bend, not break.

I run toward the parasol trees. I have no idea what a weapon powerful enough to stop a demon might look like, but it'll be somewhere nearby. I wonder if the weapon might also be looking for me. Maybe it'll make this easy and just fly into my hands or something. As I search (even though I still don't know what I'm actually searching for), the noise of the Red River trickles through the air. It's flowing again, now that Xiwangmu no longer has the prophecy paused, and I hear the clashing of steel. *Hold on!*

Desperation turns my breathing choppy as I search again where I've already searched. Could the Scroll of Chaos be wrong? There's nothing here except trees and dirt and grass. I search deeper into the parasol trees, half wishing I never had to come out again. A strange heaviness lies in the air: the weight of Chaos's power.

In my rush, I accidentally whack my clarinet against one of the trees. I glance down, heart thudding in dread at how else I might have damaged it. *It's your own fault for not putting it away properly again. What if you've broken it for good this time?*

My clarinet's gone.

Or it's more that it's *changed*. It's still a clarinet but

different. The long shape and keys are the same, but instead of wood painted black and silver keys, this clarinet's wood is left plain and pure, its grain so polished it gleams a warm chestnut. It even *feels* warm against my fingers as I hold it. The most important part? It's still untouched by grim magic.

I stare up at the parasol trees.

"Fuxi," I whisper, thinking of the demigod's myth. The way he knew to craft his musical instrument from the parasol tree because its wood was especially full of magic. And maybe playing clarinet to help with my asthma isn't exactly magic . . . except that it kind of is.

My fingers tighten around the strange new instrument. *This* is my weapon to fight Chaos. But as I look over the instrument, I notice that all the broken parts of my regular clarinet are also broken in this one. Half the ligature is still twisted off. The reed's still split. The crack that was in the bell is way longer now, climbing up nearly the entire instrument.

I can't play without fixing it first, and I have no clue how.

Numbly, stomach gone hollow, I start checking all my pockets. Like I might actually have something on me that can fix a magical weapon. It'd almost be funny if so much wasn't at stake.

I pull out a clump of orange fur from the front pocket

of my jeans. It drifts from my fingers like a feather and lands on the broken reed.

It stitches the split reed back together.

My mouth drops open as I stare at the newly fixed reed. Heart pounding wildly, I squeeze my eyes shut and picture the three drawings from the Scroll of Chaos.

A bird's wing.

A bird's head.

A feather.

Or the claw of a firebird, a terra-cotta lion head, and a clump of nian fur that could—and did—pass for a feather.

My heart's still going too fast, but now it's with excitement. I crouch down and place the clarinet on the sleeping white grass at my feet. With trembling hands, I dig out the lion head from my backpack and lay it on the grass next to the clarinet.

Terra-cotta fills up the crack like glue.

I grin. I know my magic is only a small part of this happening right now. How so much more of it is magic that's older than time—Fuxi, the parasol trees, the glorious phoenix. It's even partly the ancient dark magic of the scroll's prophecy itself for connecting everything the way it has.

After the firebird claw becomes the ligature's missing half, I go to pick up the repaired clarinet. When I touch it, its warm chestnut glow turns a ghostly white.

"No!" My mouth goes dry as I grab the clarinet. In my fingers, the wood of the instrument feels as cold as that whitened branch Sae broke off. But where the branch grew to feel warm as I held it, the clarinet doesn't at all.

I try to play a note—it comes out as a thin whistling sound. It actually sounds a lot like me when I'm wheezing my way through an asthma attack. Dread digs into my lungs and I force myself to breathe calmly. Like I have all the time in the world when I don't at all.

"Nope, not going to freak out," I mutter as I go through my backpack again, trying to find *something* that will fix the clarinet. I can't have come this far only to get stuck now. "This is all totally under control."

The immortal peach unrolls out of Marilla's pants and rolls against my fingers. My heart lurches heavily as I pick up the magical fruit. And as Xiwangmu's words come back to me, I finally understand exactly what they mean.

Remember that my gift is meant to give you what you need. It might not be the same as what you want.

Tears blur my eyes so that the peach swims into soft blotches of pink and gold. Against the bony whiteness of the clarinet—of the whole realm now under the spell of grim magic—the peach has never been more vivid or alive. It hurts to look at it, like I'm looking at the stars again. And as I stare, the truth I can see in it now hurts just as much, as hard and unbreakable as a boulder stuck in the middle of a river.

Because the truth is, saving Mom isn't going to be the kind of saving that I dreamed of. Xiwangmu gifted me the peach because I need to save Zhen, and I thought saving Zhen was how I was going to save Mom. But no matter how much I want to save her, just like how I have to fix my own qi so I can beat Chaos, Mom has to be the one to fix hers so she can get better. I can't do that for her. No one can, not really. Doctors can give the best medicine in the world, but it's still up to her to want to take them, to go to the doctors in the first place. (Which I know she does— she's seeing Dr. Gale this very week, even.) So, like the Medicine King says, I have to trust Mom to believe that she can get better. I can help her by showing her how I believe this, too. How I know Mom with depression is still Mom. How her sickness isn't who she is, but only one part of her. Mom's *always* been Mom, whether she's having good days or bad. She's never been gone, fog or not. She'll be with us for as long as she can.

I swipe at tears that keep coming. I wish badly that Marilla would suddenly show up. Not only because then I'd know she's safe, but also because then I could tell her she's always been right. Us not having all the answers doesn't have to be the worst thing in the world. I want to tell her: *We should have never stopped being scared about Mom together, not if it meant getting to feel a tiny bit braver at the same time.*

I take a deep, steadying breath, and the heaviness lifts from my chest. Not all the way, but enough; I know it'll keep getting lighter. And before Chaos can cast his spell of grim magic over the immortal peach, I set it down beside the clarinet.

The fruit shimmers, wavers, and disappears. An instant later, the clarinet wakes up, the chestnut wood shining and vivid. When I pick up the instrument, it feels even warmer than before. Or maybe it's just because my qi's finally healed and in balance. Either way, the clarinet feels full somehow. Of promise and magic and my own power. I grab my rescue inhaler from my pocket and take a long puff. I might not have super lungs yet, but I'm going to get as close as I can.

I place the clarinet's mouthpiece between my teeth and start to play.

Chaos, it's me, Astrid Xu. And I'm here to stop you.

TWENTY-THREE

The first notes of "Path of the Wind" rise into the air.

At first, it feels like I'm just playing my regular clarinet. But it's not long before I can tell the difference. This clarinet doesn't just play rich notes, it plays billionaire ones. Not just warm tones but thick honey that's melting in the sun. Echoes skip down the mountain and toward the rest of Zhen, calling all its bones to wake up.

My heart sings along. Fuxi was right about the magic of the parasol trees!

"Assssstrid!"

The shout of my name is like jumping into an ice bath, and I completely freeze. It's coming from the raging Red River down below, so loud that the entire mountain starts to quake. The forests tremble and white leaves snap off and swirl into the sky. The fields of grass around me vibrate, like giant rugs being shaken and beaten.

Chaos is here at Kunlun. He yells my name again, and the roar of his voice is just like how his shadow cloud once roared over the trees toward Marilla and me. I feel my whole body trying to shrink away and hide. My fingers slip on the clarinet keys; music skips and trips and sounds all wrong.

Chaos's voice swirls all around me, larger than life: "The realm isssss mine!"

The ground keeps shuddering: *boom, boom, boom.* It's coming from deep inside Kunlun Mountain, now a giant drum. Just as his ancestor Gonggong did to Mount Buzhou centuries ago, Chaos is smashing his powerful serpent's body against Kunlun, trying to bring it down.

Leaves start tearing free from the parasol trees. They fly into the air like they mean nothing at all, just dead things that need to be swept up. A hand-sized leaf lands at my feet and flutters there, helpless. A sharp sense of doom makes my breath catch—if even the magical parasol trees can't hold on against Chaos, how can I? This clarinet is the most powerful instrument I'll ever get to play, but right now, it feels like just a piece of wood.

"I've grown too strong, Assssstrid! I have won!"

Down below, the Red River churns and crashes. The bright high ring of clashing swords cuts through the air.

I can't stop imagining Sae swirling deep into the water and the Dragon King's army storming over Erlang and Howl. I see the water of the river start to climb while Marilla is still at the shore. I see the flood wash away Zhen and break the wheel of the world, and the spoke of the realm of Zhen snaps off and crashes into the spoke beside it. All the world's realms begin to fall one by one like a game of dominoes.

All that will happen if I can't do this.

"Asssssstrid, you should have gone home!"

Home. Mom and Dad and Marilla. Home feels so far away—*is* so far away—and I might never see it again. If I mess this up.

I tighten my grip on the clarinet, take *the* deepest breath I'm pretty sure I've ever taken, and start playing. I imagine my lungs filling with air, full and powerful and hungry. Magic in them the way magic is everywhere around me.

The air around my clarinet starts to ripple. It spreads out all around me like the world's most humongous invisible cape, the most powerful wind I've ever formed. It keeps on growing until every part of the realm is blurry through it; music sweeps down Kunlun Mountain, just as loud as Chaos's shouts.

The storm of my air paints itself outward across the realm. As it does, grim magic also begins to fade from Zhen. Colors pour into everything that was once white, like lights being plugged back in.

It's over! I want to yell at Chaos. *You've lost, so give up!*

More of the realm wakes up from the demon's spell.

The mountain's colors are splashes of the world's brightest paintings, as vivid and rich as silk. Grass as blue as the sea, moss as red as cherries, leaves as purple as plums. I aim the clarinet right at the parasol trees and their canopies glow like golden domes built out of golden stars.

A black cat darts across the grass. It's Marilla, nearly tumbling over her cat feet as she stops to gaze up at the parasol trees. She turns to me, ears flicking back and forth, and watches me play.

Don't leave, Marilla! I wish I could shout to her. From behind my clarinet, my eyes grow hot with tears. *I need to say I'm sorry. That I miss you, too.*

The ground shakes, still trying to make me fall. Chaos shouts again, smashing even harder against the mountain. "Assssstrid, stop it now! It'sssss already too late!"

I keep going, even though I can tell that my lungs are growing tired. For a second, I stop to gasp for breath.

"Just like it'sssss already too late for your mother! She'll never be free of the fog in her head! You'll never sssssee each other again!"

A whimper breaks through my gasps. "No, that's not true, I know it's not." I press a fist to my chest, trying to push away the ache there so I can breathe.

"Oh, it isssss! It's over, Assssstrid! Give up, it's over!"

More leaves of the parasol tree fall. They swirl into the

air, their gold now fringed with white. The grass beneath Marilla's paws that I already turned blue pales again, and my sister leaps away. The invisible cape of my power starts to shrink. It peels back and there's so much white again, spreading once more across Kunlun.

"Who'ssss won now?" Chaos roars. "CHAOSSSSS, THE DEMON WHO DESTROYED THE WORLD!"

I shut my eyes hard as that old panic slithers back around my heart. In my head, I see Mom standing in the doorway of my room as she listens to me practice, the way she used to before she was sick again and when I was still mostly sure of myself. Before I got too scared to keep trying. She grins at me as I miss some of the high notes. *Just keep playing, Astrid. That's what counts.*

My eyes snap open. Glaring down toward Chaos, I take a huge breath of air and shove the clarinet back into my mouth. And just keep playing.

Music spreads out once more across the realm. The wind of it rolls and rushes all around as I fight Chaos— my power now roaring, too. The parasol trees go back to being gold. That patch of grass where Marilla stood blazes bright ocean blue.

"ASSSSSTRID . . . STOP THISSSSS!"

Notes fly high over the mountain, full of my magic. There's the magic of the parasol trees in them, too, the magic of Zhen, even the delicate birdsong of phoenixes. So that together, they're louder than any demon's roar.

"STOP THIS, STOP THIS, SSSSSTOP—"

• • •

The furious shouts end. The ground beneath me gives one last heave and goes still. The canopies of the parasol trees stop shuddering. Colors race back in all the way—not a hint of white anywhere.

I can hear the Red River again. No more clanging of swords, just the low thrum of a watery current. The invisible cape falls away from the realm and I take the clarinet from my mouth.

It changes back to my regular one—black paint, the flash of silver fittings. Here's the original ligature for my mouthpiece, the reed that isn't split anymore. The crack in the bell is also gone. I nearly wish for the other clarinet to come back (I can imagine playing it at Spring Revival!, the sound of it magical even back home) but only nearly. My regular clarinet might not be made from the wood of a parasol tree, but it does still have magic of its own. It's just that I had to come here to realize it was there the whole time. That it starts with me.

The mountaintop finishes waking up, the last of Chaos's grim magic disappearing as Zhen goes free. The forests swish and rustle with the realm's magical creatures—nine-tailed foxes and black tigers, spotted deer and one-horned gazelles. I picture what must be happening at the Jade Emperor's palace, gods and goddesses blinking their eyes and shaking themselves free of a shared bad dream.

Marilla races over, and I crouch down and wait for her. Having so many things to say and not knowing how. Wishing I never knew this feeling at all.

"I thought you went down to wait for the others" is what I finally start with when she reaches me. "That would have been safer than being somewhere on your own."

She pokes the ground with her paw. I can tell she feels as weird as I do. "I was going to. But I turned back around and came up here."

"Why?"

"Because I wanted to get to the parasol trees. I knew you still needed to find the weapon to fight Chaos and were worried you couldn't."

My stomach zips up and down. If Chaos had thought to look for a black cat on the mountain instead of me . . . My eyes are hot again and I swipe at them. "I'm sorry we didn't stick together just because of a fight. I should have made sure we did, no matter what."

"Only you were meant to go all the way."

"I still wouldn't have gotten this far without your help.

It's proof of how much I needed you so that I could fight Chaos."

Marilla tries to shrug. "I had to try to help. How could I let Chaos beat my sister?"

I hug her as best I can (still considering how she's a cat). "He didn't. I'm still here."

"Xu Glue sisters?"

I nod. *Better together.*

She lets out a huge sigh, sits back, and rolls her eyes. "I actually got lost along the way. But then I heard your clarinet and that's how I knew how to get here."

"I'm still sorry." I take a deep shaky breath. "And you were right, you know? About Mom and how we can't be the ones to fix her. I promise I'll try to be more chill about it since it's not up to us, anyway." To be more like water. "And let's not fight again."

She grins. "Well, next time you make an offering to the Kitchen God, can you let me know? Even if he just keeps filtering his reports, I think it's okay to keep sending him messages. Especially if it makes us feel better."

I grin back. "Sure, that sounds good."

"We're still going to fight a lot, though."

"What? No, I'm telling you we're not going to anymore."

"We can try, but you know we'll still fight. So, let's just

really, *really* try when it comes to the big stuff. Like Mom and her getting better."

This seems like something that I should have realized, considering I'm the older sister. But whatever. "Okay, deal."

Marilla watches me with her cat eyes. "What happened with the immortal peaches?"

I start putting away my clarinet, feeling bad all over again. "It turns out stealing one wouldn't have worked out the way I thought it would. The peaches do have magic, but not the kind that can save Mom."

"That really sucks," she says softly. "I'm sorry, I wanted it to work, too. What kind of magic do they have?"

I slip on my backpack. "Magic that actually helped me beat Chaos. It made it easier to give up the peach, but I was still really scared to. Anyway, Xiwangmu was right, and now Chaos is gone for good."

She leaps at me in excitement. "You did it, Astrid! You really saved Zhen!"

I try to unclaw her from around my neck. "Not alone, though. Ouch, your claws!"

"Sorry, I keep forgetting." She sits back again. "So you're not in trouble with the Queen Mother?"

I shake my head. "No, she was really nice about it, considering she could have banished me to a mysterious realm for eternity. Or changed me into a bug."

"Gross. Oh, they're here!" Marilla jumps down to the ground.

We both watch as a travel cloud zooms across the sky. Now that they don't have our mortal weight to worry about, Sae and Erlang and Howl can travel like divine beings once more. And with their qi slowly coming back and getting rebalanced, they must be able to control their magic better, too. The puffy white travel cloud swoops along the top of the trees. It circles the mountaintop a few times before diving in low and coasting to a smooth stop over the ground.

Marilla and I run up as Sae and Erlang and Howl step off the cloud. They no longer look sick, and their grins match my own. Their power glows from around them like heat from around a sun—I didn't realize before just how strong they are. It's like realizing you're friends with secret superheroes and it's both weird and cool.

My heart pinches again, but in a good way this time. I'm so glad I'm getting to meet them the way they're meant to be.

"Erlang! Sae!" My sister bounds up to them, bumping them with her head. "Howl!" she bellows. The two of them take off, kicking up grass as they go.

Sae hugs me. "We could hear your clarinet all the way from the river. It shouldn't have been possible, and yet it was."

Erlang pats me hard on the back. "The demon felt every note like salt rubbed into a wound." He smirks. "I very much enjoyed every second of it."

I hold out my clarinet. "The weapon turned out to be another clarinet! It was made from my own using the magic from the parasol trees. The magic must have helped carry the notes extra far."

"Well, your playing helped us beat the Dragon Prince and his father's army," Sae says. "Just as your playing was ultimately Chaos's end as the prophecy promised."

"The way his serpent form simply collapsed into the river and sank away." Erlang shakes his head, smiling as he remembers the demon's defeat. "And then the Dragon Prince slinking away in shame. He's going to be in such trouble with the king. I truly wish I could be there to see it."

Sae tilts their straw basket for me to see inside. Their jade clappers are nestled among the herbs and grasses. "Safe and sound. Thank you, Astrid." Then they bow, super seriously, and Erlang does the same.

My face is red by the time they stand back up. I can't think of how you're supposed to react to famous mythological beings bowing to you, so finally I just bow back.

Beside me, a patch of air goes blurry. When it's clear again, the Queen Mother of the West stands there. Her long black hair is wilder than any painting can show, and she bares her sharp tiger teeth as she smiles at me. But I'm not scared anymore.

She gives a bow. "Zhen thanks you."

I bow back. "It was all kind of my fault, anyway. But I'm glad I could stop the flood. Everyone helped, though. I couldn't have done it myself."

"I know they did. Which doesn't change how it was still you in the end. You were very brave. Remember that."

I nod, trying to hold on to this moment for when I'm onstage again. To remember how it's okay to be scared and brave at the same time.

Xiwangmu steps closer and lowers her voice. "And I hope the immortal peach does all you hope for."

"It will. It already has, actually."

"I'm very happy to hear that." Now her eyes gleam brightly, the way a hunting animal's might in the dark. "But the next time you plan on stealing from my garden, I advise you to think twice."

I nod again, faster than I've probably ever nodded in my life. "Right."

"Hold up!" Marilla races over, cat dignity all gone as she takes in the sight of Xiwangmu. Her cat eyes are giant canary-yellow bulbs as she stares. "The Queen Mother of the West," she whispers.

It's actually kind of funny seeing Marilla starstruck.

Xiwangmu smiles and bows. "The realm thanks you as well, Marilla Xu."

"Ki-freaking-yaaah," my sister says, still whispering. She bobs low to the ground, her tail whisking back and forth. "Sure, no problem."

The air beside the Queen Mother blurs, then stills.

Standing beside her is the Jade Emperor.

TWENTY-FOUR

The Jade Emperor is tall (but not quite as tall as Erlang), with a long white mustache and a matching white beard that flows all the way down past his chin to the middle of his chest. His hat is fancier than even any of his paintings show, made out of red, jade, and gold silks. The round base is secured to his head with a red silk cord that's tied around his chin, and the rectangular board part on top is as wide as his shoulders. The board is also made out of silk, and from its four corners, beaded silk tassels hang nearly as long as his beard. The whole thing looks pretty heavy, but the emperor's robe looks like it must weigh even more, with its dozens of layers of yet more silk panels draped all over his body.

The Jade Emperor's eyes stay on Marilla and me, and I'm frozen, unable to breathe. If I thought the others glowed with magic and Xiwangmu was all queenly vibes, then the emperor's power is practically a force field around him. Mythological royalty! My mind goes blank.

"Astrid, bow!" Marilla hisses.

I do it clumsily, back to red-faced. I'm pretty sure Marilla does it twice, just in case.

"Astrid Xu," the emperor says to me, "Breaker of the Scroll of Chaos."

My face flames even hotter. "Yes, that was me. I'm sorry. I had no idea what it was."

"But once you did find out, you could have walked away. And yet you didn't, in exchange for the health of your mother. Tell me, have you been given your reward?"

"Yes." I glance over at Xiwangmu. "But it turns out it wasn't right for Mom. Her health isn't something a reward from Zhen can help. So I used it instead to help me fight Chaos by letting it help me first."

"Is that so?" He strokes one end of his long mustache. "And are you satisfied with such a reward, then?"

"Yes."

"Good. Then Zhen's debt has been paid in full. Astrid Xu, as the scroll's breaker, you were also forced to become its mender, and that role you have more than fulfilled. You stopped Chaos from destroying all of Zhen and kept the demon from replacing all our myths with his own. Time would have passed, and as time is the thief of memories, all of us here would have fully ceased to exist. Our magic and stories and who we are, no longer. For saving us, Zhen will forever be grateful." The emperor bows.

I return the bow, my face still warm.

"Marilla Xu," the emperor says next, "thank you for

accompanying your sister and for helping her defeat Chaos. The prophecy did not say such assistance would be needed, but it is true that some parts of the universe will always be spontaneous." He bows. "And I apologize that I had to make you into an animal. Your connection to our mythology isn't very strong, and my power needs that connection to bring you over whole. I assure you, you'll be human again once you're home."

"Sorry about that," Marilla mumbles. "I promise I'll work on it." If she didn't have black fur all over her face, I know she'd be red. "What made you choose a cat?"

A hint of a mischievous smile crosses the emperor's face. "It was either that or a pheasant."

Marilla sighs, remembers to bow back, then asks, sounding nearly shy: "Can I have your autograph?"

I turn to her. "Are you kidding me?" I whisper through clenched teeth.

"Autograph," the Jade Emperor repeats, his expression confused as he strokes his mustache. "What is that?"

"Your signature," Marilla says, becoming less shy by the second. "It's so we can always remember meeting you."

The emperor lifts a white brow. "You won't simply remember?"

"Well, we're mortals. We collect things like this. We

don't have actual magic, so we always try to keep souvenirs of times that *felt* magical."

He still looks skeptical but, after a moment, says, "All right, I suppose, then."

The only thing I have for him to sign is *A Handbook of Ancient Chinese Myths*. I hand it over, trying to act chill but probably doing a super bad job. "There are some blank pages in the back," I tell him.

The emperor starts to flip through the book. His eyebrows furrow as he stops at a page. "I'd argue that the Monkey King wasn't *that* clever." He flips some more. "Ha! Only eighteen levels of the realm of the dead—what happened to the rest of Diyu? Well, if I had more time, I'd go through and correct everything that might be wrong, but you and your sister need to return home." He opens the book to the back and takes the pen I find in the bottom of my backpack. He signs with an elaborate flourish, hands everything back, and I zip all of it safely into my bag.

"Can we get a selfi—" Marilla starts to ask before I remind her with a whisper that our phones don't work here.

"Ugh, you're right," she moans. "Stupid technology."

"We should probably get home now," I say, plucking her up from the ground. The sky is growing darker, the divine cloud cover now tinged with reds and oranges. Sunset.

Time won't have changed back home, but the need to be there is strong. Homesickness comes in a wave, and I miss Mom and Dad (even if they aren't able to miss us).

The emperor nods. "Erlang's power has managed to hold time still for you, but now that the threat of the scroll is over, our interference in your realm must also come to an end. In this way, too, the universe will be rebalanced."

"Thank you again for everything," I say to him and then to the Queen Mother of the West.

"We wish you a safe journey home," Xiwangmu says. She meets my eyes and smiles. "And may you and your family be well."

There's a blur of air and they both disappear.

Marilla sighs hugely. "We just saved Zhen from a demon and I can't believe we have *school* on Monday. At least we still have the whole weekend."

And I'm supposed to practice for Spring Revival! (though I'm feeling *way* better about my solo now). And I can't wait to tell Libby and Jasper everything. To show Mom and Dad the Jade Emperor's autograph and tell them how we saved a realm.

My eyes fill up as I look around at everyone. I turn to Sae and throw my arms around them. "I'm really glad you still have your special jade clappers," I say.

Sae hugs me back. "Me too. And I'll have them with me when the Eight Immortals go on our next sea journey. It's been hundreds of years since I've joined them, so I think it's time."

I step back, grinning. "Are you going to cross the East Sea again?"

"No, I think we'll explore somewhere new. We'll have to see. Thank you for helping me brave the seas once more." They take a bright yellow blossom from their straw basket. A clarity flower. "If you ever truly need us, leave it as an offering for the Kitchen God. Jun gets many requests, but he'll recognize the flower and will know what it means."

I tuck the flower carefully into one of the small protective pockets inside my backpack. "I promise we won't use it for just anything."

Before he can clap me on the back again, I hug Erlang. "I told you you'd get to rescue your mom," I say. "Make sure you tell her it was a pair of mortals who helped you."

He laughs and returns the hug. "As a demigod, I do sometimes forget that one day I'll age and weaken, as humans must. But just as my mortal father was strong, I'll still remain Erlang Shen, Zhen's greatest warrior. Thank you for reminding me of this."

"For sure."

Erlang lets go and—clapping me hard on the back—

grins. "Remember, Astrid Xu—power comes in all forms."

Marilla leaps up onto his shoulders. "I'll show you some of Bruce Lee's best moves if you ever get to come over! And I won't be a cat anymore so my kicks won't look so funny."

"If you must know, the sight was growing on me."

She paws Sae's shoulder goodbye, then jumps down and hugs Howl. "Goodbye, Howl! Doggy treats the next time we see you, promise."

I do my best to memorize everything around me. Trying to hold on to as many details as possible so I can peek into my mind and look at it whenever I want. The exact shade of gold of the parasol trees. How the grass is as blue as the ocean in summer. Everyone's faces. It's all a painting. I can already imagine its vivid silk threads, the weaving of a myth waiting to be told.

"The Battle atop Kunlun Mountain."

TWENTY-FIVE

The huge white crane glides to a stop along the ground.

I can't move right away, my arms still tight around the magical creature's neck. My body might be back on the earth again, but my mind's still soaring high over the realm, still holding on to the feeling of flying.

To be on the safe side, Sae and Erlang didn't want us crossing back over while we were still on Kunlun. They pointed out how some of the leaves in the trees and parts of the ground were still ghostly white.

"Grim magic *is* leaving the realm," Sae said, "but it's not completely gone yet. The magic of the dragon scales might yet be affected, especially using them right where Chaos's magic was centered. There's only one way we can be sure you end up exactly where you want to go."

I kept looking back as the crane lifted off from the top of the mountain. My heart felt too full as we soared toward the divine cloud cover and Sae, Erlang, and Howl slowly disappeared from view. Marilla yelled her goodbyes until way past when I knew the others could hear her, but I didn't say anything. I was too busy trying to memorize even more—the hills and forests of jade and gold, the cliffsides of purple and ivory.

Then we came out of the cloud and the rest of the realm appeared. I said a silent goodbye as we flew past everything:

See you, curling ribbon of the Red River.

Later, Weak Water, you scary gray blob.

Bye, stamp-sized Moving Sands!

Now we're landing right back where we first arrived in Zhen, and Marilla leaps out of my backpack (I left the top unzipped so she could keep her head poked out during the ride to see) onto the grassy field.

"That was *awesome!*" she says to the crane. Her tail flicks at max speed, still excited. "A thousand times better than any plane."

The crane—her name is Lin, and she's one of Xiwangmu's official attendants—tilts her beak down in a nod. "I hope it was not too rocky?"

"Nope, not at all."

I slide off Lin's back, patting her elegant neck. "Thanks again for the ride. Fly back safely!"

"You're welcome, and peaceful travels to you both." Lin takes off with a great swooping of her wings.

"Goodbye, Zhen," Marilla says as she stares out at the field and trees. The sun is nearly at the horizon. "Other than the whole must-kill-a-demon-or-the-realm-is-over thing, you were a lot of fun."

"To be fair," I say, "the non-fun part is why we're even here."

"Yeah, true. So, are you going to tell Libby and Jasper everything?"

"Maybe. I'm not sure how much of it they'll believe, though." They might believe everything because *I* believe it, and because we're friends and that's what friends do. But I also won't mind too much if they don't. I'll be more than okay if this story stays just Marilla's and mine, and Mom and Dad's.

Marilla shrugs. "Glynnis isn't into any kind of mythology, anyway."

"Oh, I almost forgot." I take out her Bruce Lee track pants and the rest of her clothes from my backpack. "You better put these on somehow or you'll be naked once we cross over."

"Which would definitely be very weird." She wades herself into the clothes until everything is kind of draped over her cat body. "All done!"

I put on my backpack and pick her up. I take two dragon scales from my jeans pocket and clutch them tightly in my hand. "Ready?"

Marilla's claws poke through the clothes wrapped

around her and into my arm. "Ready. And make sure to picture our room because we left from there, remember?"

(Erlang made sure to give us clear instructions before we left: "Think of exactly where you want to go while holding tightly to the dragon scales. You must never let go of them until you've crossed over completely."

"What happens if you do?" Marilla asked.

"You get stuck between realms." His brows lifted dramatically. "And believe us, you don't want that.")

"Got it," I say to Marilla. *Goodbye, Zhen. Thanks for all the stories.* "One . . . two . . . three!"

The world spins away and then spins back in.

We're back inside our room. The place is a mess, with everything still spilled off our desks and the furniture in the wrong places. It's exactly how a room would look if it got tilted sideways.

Marilla's back to a human ten-year-old. I'm holding her, the last sign of her short life as a cat. I let her go so I don't accidentally drop her (I've gotten way too used to carrying her around as a cat).

She pats herself all over, smiling. "I'm me again. And I'm dressed! Thank gosh."

I open my hand and look at the dragon scales on my palm. Still as shiny and green as oversized emeralds. They somehow look even more magical here in our room, with all our everyday stuff around us.

I give one to Marilla. "Where are you going to keep it?"

She walks over to her desk and puts it in the mess of her drawer. "There. Now no one can find it."

"You won't be able to, either."

"I will if I ever need it again. And I don't know if we ever will." Her mouth quavers as she thinks about how we might never see Zhen or the others again, but she heaves a sigh. "I guess whenever I start to miss them too much, I can read their myths. With you. And Mom."

I smile and tuck my own dragon scale into my backpack, into the small pocket that's also holding the hope herb from Sae. I'll decide later where to put the dragon scale for good. Somewhere safe, but also somewhere where I can look at it whenever I want.

"Do you think she's awake?" I ask. "Because we can just show her the book right now and tell her everything."

Marilla's face lights up. "*And* we can show her that we got the Jade Emperor's autograph!"

I nod. "Yes!"

"Astrid, do you think we'll forget everything one day? Like the way the Jade Emperor was saying how time is the thief of memories? It makes me sad to think I might."

The idea of forgetting even just a little bit makes something in my chest ache. But then I say (slowly, because I'm still figuring it out even as I say it), "I don't *think* we will. But even if we do, we'll still know it all happened. We have the dragon scales, remember, and the Jade Emperor's autograph. Also, I'll be better at being like water."

"I'm going to be better, too. Like let's go see Mom now!"

"Wait, let's check our phones first." I find mine from inside my backpack and look at the clock. It shows two minutes after the time it first got stuck. Time is working again here.

"Mine's good, too." My sister holds out her phone for me to see. "Erlang remembered to start time back up."

"He did."

We exchange newly glum looks, both of us still in Zhen with all its magic and power. But then I start thinking about how excited Mom's going to be to hear about everything, and I'm already super curious if anyone in band class is going to notice on Monday that I won't be coasting anymore. Marilla's checking to see if she got any texts, and I bet she's making plans with Glynnis for the weekend (which reminds me that I'm supposed to text Libby and Jasper).

I glance around our room. "Do you think we should clean up first?"

"Nah. We can fix it all before bed. After dinner and movie night."

"Okay." I take *A Handbook of Ancient Chinese Myths* from my backpack. I also grab the hope herb from the small pocket inside and tuck it into the pages of the book. "Ready!"

"I'm just going to check on Dad to see if he noticed anything weird while we were gone," Marilla says. "I mean, Chaos *was* slowly stealing Erlang's qi. Then I'll ask him if we can get sushi for dinner!"

"I vote for Korean."

"We just had that."

"No, we had sushi last. You just don't remember."

"Mexican, then."

I give her a look. "Just because we agreed that we can still argue about small stuff doesn't mean you should get to pick."

"You just picked Korean!"

"I said I *voted* for it."

"Aaah!" Marilla heads for the door. "We'll ask Mom and Dad to pick, then. I'll meet you in Mom's room!" She races out into the hall.

I head over and knock at the door really quietly, just in case. But she calls for me to come in, and I step inside, book clutched to my chest.

"Hi, Mom," I say.

She's still in bed. "Astrid." She blinks at me, puzzled. "Weren't you just here?"

I notice the drapes are pulled open when they weren't before; spring light comes in. It might be Dad who came in to do it, but I think it was Mom. Maybe after I read her the myth of Shennong and left the room, she suddenly felt the urge to see again and got out of bed—not because I was the reason, but because *she* was. And it might be foggy again tomorrow, but right now it's clear, and early evening sunshine glows in through the window. It feels good.

"Sorry," I say, "but I really wanted to show you something. Marilla and I both do, I mean. She's going to be here in a second."

"Can it wait? Isn't Dad almost done with work?"

"He is. But it can't wait. I bet Dad wouldn't even want us to."

She slowly sits up, a small smile on her face. "Okay, what's going on?"

"We just need to wait for Marilla." I go and leave the hope herb on her bedside table. "I'll tell you about this afterward. It's also a part of what we have to show you."

"You girls aren't in trouble, are you?"

"We're not." I sit down on the bed. "I'm doing really good on my clarinet for Spring Revival!, by the way. For my solo part. You don't have to worry about me."

"I'm so glad to hear that. And I'm going to try really

hard to be there, okay?" She studies me. "I was never worried about you and clarinet. Not any more than I worry about Marilla and track, know what I mean? I just want you girls to do the best you can and have fun, too."

"I think . . . I just want you to not worry about me so that you can spend all your energy on yourself. To get better." I toy with the pages of the book. "I also know that you and Dr. Gale and your other doctors are all trying really hard to get you better, too. I guess I always knew that. I just thought I could also help."

"You *do* help, exactly as you are." She holds my hand. "It's not your job to do more. Or Marilla's or Dad's. It's mine, just like you said."

I nod. "It's just really different than how I thought I could help. But it's okay, I'll get used to it." I smile. "So, for now I'll practice and get so good that I'll be able to handle any solo. And if you can't go to Spring Revival!, then I can show you at Summer Kick-Off."

"Is Mrs. Battiste already working on that? My goodness, she is prepared."

"She's not, but I am."

Mom squeezes my hand tighter. "I'll aim for both. I promise."

It's another promise while she's sick, but it's easier to believe her this time. "Sounds good."

She taps a finger on *A Handbook of Ancient Chinese Myths* and I hand it over. "This is the same book you had earlier, right?" She begins to flip through it. "The one you said Raj dropped off?"

"Yes! But wait, don't look through it yet." I glance impatiently at the door. "I just need Marilla to hurry up—"

"Oh, there's handwriting in the back!" Mom sits up straighter and holds out the book for me to see. "It seems to be another myth, but it's not one I'm familiar with. I wonder who added it in here?"

Heart fluttering, I stare down at the page. It's full of elegant handwriting—the *Jade Emperor*'s handwriting.

A knock at the door. Marilla bursts in. "Hi, Mom! You'll never guess what happened to Astrid and me today!"

I turn to look at my sister. I can't stop grinning. "Marilla, you have to read this!"

So we do.

The Mortal Girl Who Saved a Realm

Once, there was a mortal girl named Astrid who lived in the mortal world of Countries and Continents. She had many interests, such as playing clarinet and learning about Chinese mythology. She also had many worries, such as making a mistake at her next concert and how she was always fighting with her sister, Marilla. There was also her mother's illness, which Astrid worried about most of all.

One day, she accidentally set a terrible prophecy into motion, which was that a magical realm named Zhen would soon be destroyed by a terrible demon. To fix this, Astrid herself would have to be the one to vanquish the demon. Sent to Zhen to accomplish this task, Astrid—being a mortal without magic now in a realm known for that very thing—was given assistance. She gained the aid of a magician, a warrior, and the warrior's loyal battle dog. She had the help of Marilla, who was transported to Zhen alongside Astrid and who took on the form of a black cat. Also whisked along was Astrid's musical instrument, her clarinet.

Of course, destroying the demon was such a dangerous task that Astrid was offered a reward—an immortal peach to cure her mother. Astrid accepted, and so the quest began.

The deadly obstacles she had to overcome:

Birds that burned like the sun.

A pit of sand that swallowed everything up.

A herd of charging beasts.

Water that drank up even shadows.

With the help of all her companions, Astrid managed to beat all these obstacles. And with each accomplishment, Astrid herself changed and grew.

She strengthened her lungs, and so her worry over her concert shrank a bit.

Working together made her and Marilla understand each other more, and so they agreed to no longer waste their time fighting so much.

Astrid also realized that the best way to help her mother was to show her mother how much she was trusted and loved, and how Astrid believed in her strength, illness and all.

Put together, all these changes made Astrid so powerful she became capable of her own kind of magic, magic she wielded through her clarinet. The seed of that power had long been planted, but in Astrid's changing and growing, her power was finally able to grow, too.

Soon, it was time for her final task, which was to destroy the demon on the top of the great mountain of Kunlun. Using her newfound power along with the sacrifice of her reward, the immortal peach, Astrid eventually defeated the demon by drowning out his roar with her music.

After returning to her mortal land of Countries and Continents, Astrid could no longer hold on to all her new power and magic—as a mortal, such a thing was not possible. But not all her power and magic would leave her. And over time, some of it would come to touch others in her life.

But that is another myth for another day.

Author's Note

This novel discusses and explores the impact of mental illness on a family. While the setting of an ancient Chinese realm steeped in mythology is a fictional one, living with a loved one's mental illness is a very real struggle within many families, and I felt Astrid's story an important one to share.

For readers with questions about depression and mental illness, please reach out to a trusted adult for further guidance. For resources on mental health awareness and support, here are some that might be helpful for both readers and parents:

United States
Anxiety & Depression Association of America: www.adaa.org
Child Mind Institute: www.childmind.org
National Alliance on Mental Illness: www.nami.org
National Institute of Mental Health: www.nimh.nih.gov

Canada
Centre for Addiction and Mental Health: www.camh.ca
Kids Help Phone: www.kidshelpphone.ca
Wellness Together Canada: www.wellnesstogether.ca

Acknowledgments

My deepest and most heartfelt thanks to my agent, Victoria Marini, and my editor, Orlando Dos Reis. Also many thanks to Christina Chung, Matt Ringler, Janell Harris, Jessica White, Jody Corbett, Lori Lewis, Priscilla Eakeley, and everyone at Scholastic who helped bring Astrid to life.

Thank you always to my family, especially Jesse, Matthew, and Gillian.